PENGUIN METRO READS
OH YES, I'M SINGLE!

Durjoy Datta was born in New Delhi. He completed a degree in engineering and business management before embarking on a writing career. His first book, *Of Course I Love You . . .*, was published when he was twenty-one years old and was an instant bestseller. His successive novels—*Now That You're Rich . . .*, *She Broke Up, I Didn't!*, *Oh Yes, I'm Single!*, *If It's Not Forever . . .*, *Someone Like You*—have also found prominence on various bestseller lists, making him one of the highest-selling authors in India. Durjoy lives in New Delhi, loves dogs and is an active CrossFitter.

For more updates, you can follow him on Facebook (www.facebook.com/durjoydatta1) or Twitter (@durjoydatta).

Neeti Rustagi was born in New Delhi, and has worked in the hospitality industry for over ten years. *Oh Yes, I'm Single! . . .* is her first book. She lives in Australia with her husband. She can be reached on Facebook or email at neetirustagi@gmail.com.

Also by Durjoy Datta

Hold My Hand

*

She Broke Up, I Didn't!
I Just Kissed Someone Else!

*

Of Course I Love You
Till I Find Someone Better

(With Maanvi Ahuja)

*

Now That You're Rich
Let's Fall In Love

(With Maanvi Ahuja)

*

Till the Last Breath . . .

*

Someone Like You

(With Nikita Singh)

*

You Were My Crush
Till You Said You Love Me!

(With Orvana Ghai)

*

If It's Not Forever
It's Not Love

(With Nikita Singh)

DURJOY   NEETI
DATTA   RUSTAGI

Oh Yes, I'm Single!

AND SO IS MY GIRLFRIEND!

Penguin
metro reads

PENGUIN METRO READS

Published by the Penguin Group

Penguin Books India Pvt. Ltd, 11 Community Centre, Panchsheel Park, New Delhi 110 017, India

Penguin Group (USA) Inc., 375 Hudson Street, New York, New York 10014, USA

Penguin Group (Canada), 90 Eglinton Avenue East, Suite 700, Toronto, Ontario, M4P 2Y3, Canada (a division of Pearson Penguin Canada Inc.)

Penguin Books Ltd, 80 Strand, London WC2R 0RL, England

Penguin Ireland, 25 St Stephen's Green, Dublin 2, Ireland (a division of Penguin Books Ltd)

Penguin Group (Australia), 707 Collins Street, Melbourne, Victoria 3008, Australia (a division of Pearson Australia Group Pty Ltd)

Penguin Group (NZ), 67 Apollo Drive, Rosedale, Auckland 0632, New Zealand (a division of Pearson New Zealand Ltd)

Penguin Books (South Africa) (Pty) Ltd, Block D, Rosebank Office Park, 181 Jan Smuts Avenue, Parktown North, Johannesburg 2193, South Africa

Penguin Books Ltd, Registered Offices: 80 Strand, London WC2R 0RL, England

First published in India by Grapevine India Publishers 2011
Published in Penguin Metro Reads by Penguin Books India 2013

Copyright © Durjoy Datta 2013

ISBN 9780143421580

Typeset in Adobe Caslon Pro by Eleven Arts, Delhi
Printed at Manipal Technologies Ltd, Manipal

Dedicated to all the nerds who were laughed at in high school . . . since I was one of them!

Author's Note

This book borrows heavily from the incidents narrated to me by Durjoy. The names have been changed in the book to spare some people the embarrassment. Therefore, any resemblance to real life people and incidents is intentional.

Names of books, people, places and timelines have been changed to avoid *fatwa*s and death threats. Despite all these hiccups and denials from Durjoy's side, all the incidents in the book are true to the best of my knowledge and memory.

—*Neeti Rustagi*

It Isn't a Love Story!

People write love stories, and people write autobiographies. People write autobiographies that revolve around love stories. And more often than not, these love stories are picture perfect. Girl meets boy, boy eyes girl, girl looks at her friends for approval and gets it, girl reciprocates, silent sighs, sleepless nights, first kiss, a few more sleepless nights, they go against the world and everything falls into place. *Boring*.

I mean, wouldn't you rather be lying in the arms of your loving boyfriend or girlfriend in the backwaters of Kerala or Mauritius depending on how lucky you are or how rich your partner is, than reading this book on a Friday night, curled up in your bed with no one to cuddle but your pillow.

But the fact is that you are *here*, and in all probability know that finding true love is as difficult as finding a needle in a haystack. But then again, love wouldn't be such a huge concept and Valentine's Day would just be another day if love was something you could find walking on the subway, or over the counter. Love is not something which you can receive by an email whenever you need it; it is tough finding love. For guys, it's a little easier—give them a nice smile on a nice body

1

and they can fool themselves that they are in love, for a little while at least.

Anyway, as we go finding true love, we all experience turbulence, speed bumps, ugly turns, tears, tonnes of ice cream, assholes, bitches . . . but do we stop? We do not. We fall in love repeatedly, hoping that things will turn out just fine this time, and more often than not, they do not. However, if they do, it makes for a great love story. What if it does not?

This book is about when it *almost* doesn't. And some other unrelated things. Is this my story? No. But it's the story of someone I know, in his own words. He has been around for six years, and has led one of the strangest love lives I have come across. He has rarely been single and has always been a sucker and a staunch supporter of true love. He has dumped and been dumped countless times. This guy just keeps falling in and out of love. People get into flings knowing that it is going to be a fling. This guy gets into it thinking it's a relationship and only when it's over, he comes out, scratches his head and says. *'Oh, it was a fling!'*

He always believes that love is waiting right around the corner! It will come when it comes; the possibilities are endless.

For him, it has come. *Lucky bastard.*

This book is his story. That lucky bastard is Joy, my best friend.

✳✳✳

'Joy . . . So, now that you finally know what you had been looking for, let's go for it.'

'Go for what?' Joy said as he casually sat with his legs up on the coffee table.

'Tell me all of it. Everything. From the first girl,' I said. 'You had promised you would!'

'NEETI, for the last time around—NO! Firstly, it is boring, not to mention—embarrassing. And secondly, find some other scapegoat for your book!' he said as he pushed me aside to watch a repeat of a soccer match. I snatched the remote and turned it off, inviting a nasty look from him.

'It's the first time that I have asked you for something,' I said, with my puppy face look. We, girls, are lucky to have such a weapon, aren't we? Moreover, Joy usually fell for it. As he did that day.

'Fine. Fine,' he said. 'But I will change names. I will change things as I deem fit. And no details. Maybe I will even lie and exaggerate, and make myself to be a stud instead of the raging nerd that I am. And I will rush through it. She'll be coming any moment and we are going out. And I am not doing this again.'

'Why? That's unfair. You have all the time for your girl and not for me. I knew you before you got to know her, you were my friend

3

before you became her boyfriend. Hmmphff. . .' I faked anger. 'Take it or leave it!' he said.

'Whatever.'

Though my displeasure was evident, he did not budge from his decision, and frankly speaking, I didn't really have much of a problem; I had his attention now.

With a couple of coffees and bagels at hand, he started on the story.

'Tell me everything,' I said.

'Fine. Neeti . . . It was 1996. And . . .' Joy started. 'It's a long time back, so I may miss some things and make up stuff that I don't remember. . .'

And then Joy started narrating the story. His story. And hers.

* * *

The First Crush

It was 1996. And I was in the eighth standard. Girls weren't pulling down socks to flaunt their legs yet. Guys were still to discover the wonders of hair gels. And girls were still not their top priority. We were all busy sprinkling ink on each other's shirts and sharing lunches. The happy pre-puberty days.

And that's exactly when I met *her*. I saw the face, which imprinted itself on my brain for many years to come. Well, to be true, I didn't meet her, not exactly. I just saw her across the room full of rowdy and shouting eighth-standard students.

'Nisha?' the teacher had called out.

'Yes, ma'am,' she had responded in her chirpy voice.

How did she look?

She was like the first breeze of autumn, like the sparkling sun after a long cold night; she was a midsummer night's dream. She barely came up to my shoulders, her eyes were darker than the blackest night, her soft pink lips seemed to be made out of candy, her cute steps across the floor, as she walked around, would make my day. I still remember her perfectly well in our school uniform with a pink muffler around her neck. And the reddish winter glow on her cheeks. *Ah!*

How did I look?

I was fat, dark and ridiculously *ugly*. Like. Totally. Ugly. It was as if God had something against me. If he had to make me so ugly, he should have played with my mind too and made me have a crush on someone as ugly as I was, someone with freckles and unruly hair, maybe a lazy eye! Why her? Why Nisha? Why the cutest, chirpiest girl in the class?

Anyway, seven years later, in the winter of 2003, I had just turned eighteen. It was my last year in school and somehow, I had managed to grow even fatter and uglier, and she had only grown prettier. She was no longer the girl I had first seen seven years back. She had grown positively womanly, if you know what I mean. She was cute then, but she was *irresistibly* beautiful now. Her lips had grown pinker, her eyes were wider and they sparkled even more now, her hair was now long and worn in a style far beyond her age. All these years the gap between her social standing and popularity and mine had just kept widening. Although I had grown taller and she was still short and hopped around like a pocket-sized bunny, it didn't make her any less un-gettable.

It was the last year and I was in the S.A. dilemma.

What is a Screwed Anyway *dilemma?*

It's something that almost every guy has faced in his lifetime. It's almost as common as the Asshole Boyfriend phenomenon.

What is the Asshole Boyfriend *phenomenon?*

It's when every girl you like eventually ends up going out with the guy you hate. Simple, right?

Now back to the Screwed Anyway dilemma.

The girl is out of your league—but she is single—you ask her out—she refuses—you are screwed!

The girl is out of your league—and she is single—someone else asks her out—you are screwed!

Now the good news about the first one is that you don't feel choked about your feelings and you don't regret that you didn't tell the person you love about how you felt about them. And I just had to tell her! Never give in to this feeling, nothing comes out of telling the person you love that you love him or her. It's *bullshit*, it's an urban legend. After doing it, you realize it's better to live on the tiny hope that maybe she loved you, rather than being rejected and humiliated outright. But I was just an ugly, fat kid. What did I know about these complexities? All I knew was that she was the girl of my dreams and I liked her to bits.

Let's just rewind a bit to tell you what had happened in the last seven years of my *secret* relationship with Nisha, a relationship about which Nisha herself knew nothing about.

I loved her like crazy.

Within the first week of seeing her, I knew her phone number, the street she lived on, what her parents did, what bus route she took, almost everything there was to be known about her! Though, getting all this information seems regular right now, the year was 1996 and things were different back then!

As time went by, my obsession escalated. After a year, and for the next seven years, I walked two kilometres every day after school so that I could share the same bus route. For the next seven years, I always took two schoolbags so that I could take a seat in two rows and decide later which row would give me a clearer view of her, after she took her seat. I did these things on a very regular basis, and now that I think of it, I guess I should have gone to a doctor instead.

Anyway, back then I wasn't a big extrovert, but by the time 2003 came along, I had retreated so far into my shell that I had problems even engaging in everyday conversations with people. *Why did that happen?*

My obsession, now at dizzy levels, made me believe that Nisha would hear every word I say, and that I needed to measure my words before saying them out loud. And that is when, deep down, I knew for certain, that a girl like her, who hung around with cooler kids with gel in their hair and motorcycles parked outside the school, wouldn't even give a passing thought to someone like me. She had a whole army of *better* boys who catered to her every whim and fancy; she was a pampered kid. Had it been left to me, I would have carried her around in my schoolbag to prevent her from the torture of walking.

Man! I *did* need to go to a psychiatrist back then. But it was around that time that I realized that I was getting a little overboard, that it was just a crush and I had to get over it, especially since my grades had started to slip to unacceptable levels. I started to concentrate a little more on my engineering entrance examinations, putting everything else aside for a little while. It did soften my preoccupation with her. Sometimes I thought it would have been a lot easier for me, had she started going out with somebody. But that's just pure speculation; I might just have killed myself, metaphorically speaking.

I clearly remember; it was the last week of our school when I mustered up the courage to go to her, my heart in my mouth, readying myself up for rejection. It was mostly out of panic because I felt I would *never* see her again. Who knew Facebook would burst into the scene in three years and you would always be in touch with friends you never wished you had!

Anyway, she was almost set to go to some college in Delhi University, surrounded by boys and girls as cute as she was, and I was keeping my fingers crossed for my entrance examinations. I just *had* to tell her. I couldn't have chosen a worse time, though. It was only later that it came to my knowledge that there were three more guys, all of whom were better than I was (because being *worse* than me was kind of impossible), who had asked her out around those very days; all of them were turned down.

'Umm . . . err . . . hi . . .' I said.

She smiled as she always did and said, 'Hi, Joy.'

She fucking knows my name! She fucking knows my name! Obviously she does, you asshole. You have shared the same class since you didn't even know what an erection was.

'Hi,' I said and shut up. I started rubbing my palms together which were sweating by now. I shivered. This was the best moment in our seven-year-long *secret* relationship. We had finally said *Hi*, our first real conversation.

'Yes?' she said, still smiling.

'Umm . . . nothing . . . I just wanted to tell you that . . . that . . . I think you are very nice . . .' I said. My face flushed red and my head spun.

Yes, in those days, *nice* and *cute* were the only words we all used. Asking a girl out was a *really* big deal and it took only a stud or a man crazed with love to do it. Having a girlfriend was unheard of, like a myth, something that only happened in movies, or in colleges.

'Well . . . thank you,' she said and smiled. 'Joy, I need to go. I will talk to you later.'

'S . . . sure,' I mumbled as she walked away from me. I *wasn't* screwed. She was still single. I had told her what I wanted to . . . almost, and she had smiled. I was a *winner*!

My happiness was shortlived; a few minutes later, I saw her talking to a few of her friends in the corner. I didn't know whether it was just my mind playing games with me, but I saw her pointing at me and smiling, and her friends were laughing.

Maybe, they were right in doing so. I had been fool enough to have a glimmer of hope that something would come out of me telling Nisha that I liked her. I turned away from them and spent the next two hours in the washroom crying like a little girl. And felt *disgusted* with myself.

I tried to erase the memory of that incident ever since. But it only deepened the inferiority complex and exacerbated my fear of talking to girls. The incident kept reminding me that I was ugly . . . and worthless, and that I wasn't fit to be loved by any girl.

Though two days later, on the farewell night, I got a picture clicked with her, my first with a girl, and every time I look at that blurred picture today, I think of her. And the day she smiled . . .

And when her friends had laughed at me.

Things changed thereafter. Pretty drastically.

***

'That's it? That's your first crush? You never even got to talk to her properly?' I asked.

'Yes,' Joy said as he fished out the photograph from the school farewell album. He looked at it for a while and passed it over to me.

'Oh . . . this is a terrible photograph.' I said. The photograph had creases and thumb imprints all over it.

'That's because I have thrown and then retrieved it more than once from various dustbins over a period of time. I was in love with her even after we left school. I tracked her whereabouts for quite some time. But then, she started seeing someone, and slowly I lost interest,' he said as he looked over my shoulder at the picture.

'. . . and you look terrible here,' I said. 'You really were ugly, Joy!'

'Thank you for pointing that out. You are such a great friend.'

'She is very cute, though. It's not your fault that you didn't get her.' I turned it around and read what he had written in his own handwriting.

When I see any couple, I see you and me . . . us, together until the end,
When I feel the wind on my face, I sense your breath,
When I feel the warmth of the winter sun,
I miss the confinement of your arms,
When I cross a road, I yearn to hold your hand,

11

When I hear my name, it sounds incomplete when it doesn't
have your voice!
You've taken me over totally and I have surrendered myself
wilfully to you . . .

'It's very nicely written,' I said. 'For an eighteen-year-old.'

'I know. I was nuts. Anyone would be,' he sighed. 'She was very cute. The kind of cute you would see naked and still not be turned on by it, she was that cute, like a naked teddy bear.'

'Isshh, that's gross! And I don't even know if it's a compliment!' I said.

'What makes you think it's not a compliment!'

'It's not. I will feel insulted if someone sees me . . . you know . . . and is not . . . whatever . . . Anyway. Continue.'

Joy smoothed out the picture and put it back in the album, took a deep breath and said, 'I didn't get through any of the engineering exams that year. As if I didn't already feel like I was the dumbest, ugliest bastard, I had to screw up my exams too.'

The First Love

I didn't get through any of the engineering exams that year, and I blamed it on my obsession with Nisha. So the next one year, I spent at home and prepared for the exams, which I should have cleared the first time around.

It is strange to think of it now, but I had totally lost touch with everybody. My old classmates had started to go to college and moved on with their lives, and to be very frank, I was *never* very popular amongst my friends; I had like two friends and they weren't friends, they were more like study partners. They promptly forgot me, and I forgot them. It worked for me though for it gave me more time to bury myself in Quantum Physics and Integration.

Sitting at home, I was getting even fatter; eating was the only way out of the labyrinth of self-pity and depression and loneliness. After six months of staying at home, I weighed close to ninety kilograms and our family physician told me I would soon be obese and diabetic. My mom, concerned and panicked, thinking it was her fault that her son was flabby and dying, put me on a healthy diet and forced me to jog every morning.

Although I hated fruits and sweating in my tracksuit every morning, six months later, I was lighter by twenty pounds. I was still was pretty *heavy*—weighed around eighty kilograms in a five-ten frame—that was still better than weighing a hundred and ten.

Soon, I cleared the engineering college entrance examinations. College started on a diametrically different style than how school had ended. All my jeans were loose now, so they hung low. And unintentionally, I was among the first ones in college to have caught on to the low-waist baggy jeans phenomenon that had just hit the country!

Nobody knew now what an ugly nerd I used to be. Ugly, I still was, but not as nerdy as I used to be. Everyone took me as a quiet well-dressed guy; some people mistook my quietness as attitude, and they said I was a snob, something that I didn't mind.

Weeks later, I found myself hanging around with the coolest, hippest people in the college although more often than not, I found myself out of place as I lacked the skill to converse! I had never talked to people. I didn't know the places they hung out. And I never spent money on recreation. I was a *misfit*.

'Man! Why don't you say something?' Arnab said, miffed that I had stood there like a dumb statue while he was talking to two girls from the dance team of our college. He, on the other hand, had been doing a remarkable job at keeping them entertained. They had kept giggling and laughing at his stupid small jokes. And frankly, I was a little jealous.

Who was Arnab?

I had known him for long . . . he had been in another section in our school and though I was sure he didn't know I existed, I knew all about him. House Captain, captain of the football team et cetera . . . Though he was not very remarkable looking, he was certainly one of the smartest people I had ever met. He was one of the few guys in our school who had a girlfriend.

'I didn't have anything to say,' I said.

'Such an attitude doesn't work with a girl, man! I know they weren't hot or anything, but they weren't very bad either. You should have talked to them!' he said.

What he thought was *attitude*, was actually sheer inability. He had no idea how badly I wanted to be like him. Centre of attention of all the girls, great conversational skills, the stupid jokes, the works . . . I wanted all that. Desperately.

'Anyway, I need to talk to you,' he said and led me to the canteen. 'You know about Sarah, don't you?'

Sarah? Who didn't? Sarah was the goddess of our batch and another claim to fame for Arnab. They had been dating since the last three years and everybody knew about them. Sarah's short skirts, long never-ending legs and Arnab's achievements were like daily news for us in school.

'Yes. I do,' I said, as my mind raced with images of Sarah in the short school skirt and the snugly fitting shirt. She was one of the first girls I had seen a tattoo on. On her left leg. She always made sure her socks were pulled down and her scorpion tattoo peeked out. Guys used to line up outside her class whenever she sat on the first seat, just to see her legs glisten in the sunlight that poured in through the windows; her body was one of the most talked about in hushed tones amongst boys and girls alike. Her hair was always in a studied mess, as if she had just woken up after a night of rough lovemaking. The slight brownish streaks in her hair only made her more desirable.

'When we were in school, everything was fine . . . I mean it still is,' Arnab said. 'I still care about her, she is very sweet and nice and I can't see her cry or anything, but I think I need to break up with her,' he added in his guilt soaked voice. This was 2004, these things happened. Guys thought *twice* before breaking up.

'Umm . . . why?' I asked, puzzled.

'You have had girlfriends, right?' he said. 'You know how it is. After a while, it just fizzles out. The excitement is just not there anymore'

'Yes,' I said.

I had no idea what he was talking about, but I lied. I didn't want to tell him that I was yet to have a proper conversation with a girl. Plus, now that I had stopped dressing up in hideous trousers with sports shoes or brown open-toed sandals, it was almost believable that I might have had a girlfriend in school.

'I am just *bored*. Plus there is so much to see here. I mean the girls here. They are cute, and I am getting all their attention, I can't lose out on that. And Sarah has a problem when I hang out with them, it's very stifling and restricting. And of late, she has been so possessive. All she says is that ever since we have left school, all I think about is college, and it's so irritating,' he said.

Obviously, I didn't know what to say to that. I wish I could tell him that all I wanted to do was to have a bunch of kids with Sarah and keep her away from the world because she was so god darn hot, but I decided to go with something *cooler*.

'Break up with her,' I said, as dispassionately as I could.

'Yes! That's what. Everyone has been telling me otherwise. But I knew you would say something different. You get me. Those fucking nerds, I tell you. I mean, Sarah is good, but I can get *better*, right? This is college! I've got to move on.'

'Yes, you do!' We shook hands and smiled at each other.

I patted myself on the back. I was *not* a nerd. Certified

by someone who himself wasn't. Red-letter day for me. *He's breaking up with Sarah! He's crazy!*

A week later, he broke up with her. Many conversations followed, and though he never wanted to go back to her, he often felt guilty and sad about the whole incident. In the next few days, I knew everything about their relationship. Sarah used to call up Arnab and remind him of all the times they had spent together in an attempt to get him back. But Arnab didn't budge. It was *cool* to have broken up. *I* had told him that. I—the cool guy who had never ever had a conversation with a girl.

Though I have to admit that the day he told me that they had kissed, I was shocked. (*Let me remind you again—2004.*) For many days after that, I had replaced him in the kissing scene with myself and fantasized about Sarah.

'You have *kissed*?' I asked, shell-shocked.

'So? I am sure you have, too,' he said.

'Umm . . . yeah . . . but . . . then you shouldn't have broken up so brutally.'

'What?' he said. 'We have done other things beyond that too . . . but I am not going to tell you that.' He nudged me with his elbow and smirked at me. He looks stupid; I am a mix of shocked and jealous and nauseous.

'*What?* What have you done?' I asked, almost sweating.

'I won't tell you. And neither would she,' he said.

'But won't her next boyfriend mind?' I said, innocently. I forgot to be cool. How could I have been cool? The guy in front of me was hinting that he had seen his super-hot girlfriend, like, *without her shirt, or whatever!* I was freaking out. Or something close to that. My mind was in shambles.

'She won't tell the next guy, for sure . . .'

'Who knows?' I said. I figured it was the right thing to say, remembering suddenly that I wasn't a nerd anymore, except that I really was. I reminded myself that I had kissed and done *stuff*, and with time, I had started believing in my own lies. My false confidence had gone sky high, and I had started using words like *fuck, fucking, asshole, fuck it* with unmatched gusto, as the popular kids did.

Days passed and Arnab got increasingly irritated with Sarah's calls and her constant crying. Often, I used to pick up her call and tell her that Arnab was busy somewhere. I should mention here that Sarah was the *first* girl I ever talked to, over the phone; the first few times were terrifying.

And then, Sarah asked for my number. She knew I would be the only one who would know about Arnab's whereabouts.

'Joy?' I could barely hear her amidst all the sobs.

'Sarah?' I said. I looked at the watch. It was eleven-thirty. Night calling, I guessed. Those were the days when a minute of extra day calling cost two bucks. I was whispering for I didn't want to wake my parents up; I wondered if they could hear Sarah's sobs over the phone.

'Is Arnab going out with somebody? Please don't lie to me.'

'Arnab? No!' I said. I had realized that talking over the phone was a lot easier because no one is staring at my hideous face, no one is noticing how I shift my feet, or how I look here and there and look like I am going to faint.

'Then why isn't he picking up my calls?' she asked, still crying.

'He must be busy.'

'Stop defending him. He was never this busy earlier. Not a single message the entire day? *No* one can be that busy!' she said.

'I don't know what to say . . .'

From there on, I didn't have to say too much. *Eight hours.* Eight straight hours, she went about every detail in their relationship. Hour by hour, day by day and month by month. She conveniently skipped some portions, the kisses and *stuff* portions, but apart from that she missed nothing.

Though there was a lot of crying and sobbing and consoling in the entire phone call, it was my first received phone call from a girl and I enjoyed every moment of it. For the first time, I realized how soothing a girl's voice was, even seductive at times. Well, *most* of the times!

The following morning, I was greeted by an enthusiastic and an extremely happy Arnab.

'Hey!' he said.

'Hi . . .'

'Thank you, man! For talking to her. I think I can finally breathe easy. If you talk to her, I am sure she will do the crying in front of you and save me the pain of going through it every day.'

'Hmmm . . .' I smirked.

'Sorry, if she troubled you too much!' he apologized, as he shook my hand.

He walked away and I pressed the *send* button. It was our thirtieth exchanged text that day, Sarah and I. She had just texted me that she was waiting for the clock to strike eleven so that she could talk to me again. I had replied with a smiley.

A girl wants to talk to me. That was another first. Usually, girls only wanted to get away from me, or pretend that I didn't exist.

For the next one week, the same schedule followed. We exchanged texts throughout the day about how our day was going, every single detail . . . and it was strange how interested she was in what I had to say; it was another first, someone was interested in my life. It was also my first tryst with writing. They were only texts, though some used to be really long, but Sarah was the first one to tell me that I wrote well. I never texted using shortened words and she liked that.

And at nights, she talked about how devastated she was; she couldn't stop talking about the break-up.

And after a few days, I no longer sweated when I talked to her. It had started coming to me naturally. She once said that I almost sounded like Arnab . . . and that was why she talked to me. Though that was a little derogatory, it still sounded like a compliment to me, at least initially.

Days passed by and though we hadn't even met, I started getting possessive about her and asked her to stop telling me how much I reminded her of Arnab. I even asked her to stop talking about Arnab all the time. Things were getting *serious* from my side. It wasn't love, but there were territorial issues. Sarah was my territory now. And I hated to imagine that Arnab was still around anywhere near.

'You think we should meet sometime?' I said.

Words now came to me naturally. I was getting better. I could make her smile, make her laugh her guts out, make her feel better . . . all by *talking*. At least, I had finally started to realize, that talking to the opposite sex wasn't exactly rocket science. Though sometimes, it was really hard not to get, like, a little turned on when she used to whisper on the phone. Sometimes I found myself thinking about what it would be like to kiss her, just as Arnab had. I often imagined the two of us on the last seat of an empty classroom, in her school uniform, the short skirt and the tight shirt, her inviting smile and the irresistible pout would call out to me. *Goosebumps.*

'Sure, we should,' she said. 'We should have met even before I met Arnab,' she said flirtatiously. So. Totally. Hot.

The day when I had to meet her finally came; she wasn't sure at first whether she should meet me but then she said she really wanted to see me in person. I was shivering in my pants. I had never been out with a girl alone. I didn't know how to keep them entertained. I remembered the time when I wouldn't even dare to look at her long enough, let alone talk to her. But things were *different* now, I told myself.

That day, it took me more than two hours to get ready. It included brushing twice, changing my shirt thrice, changing my shoes, forgetting my wallet at home . . . et cetera. My pocket money used to be a paltry sum of six hundred bucks and I did a mental calculation over a hundred times as to whether it would be enough or not.

We were to watch a movie together; it was my plan. A dark movie hall to hide my fidgety self and Dolby-surround sound noise to drown out my stammering speech. That's what I needed first . . . just to get my confidence going, before I could look into her eyes and talk.

I reached the Cineplex exactly five minutes before the movie was scheduled. I didn't want to spend too much time outside trying to make conversation with her. She still hadn't reached. *Jackpot!*

I bought the tickets and stood at the gate. Within the next thirty seconds, she came and smiled at me. We were frisked and rushed in. Not a word exchanged. Not a look exchanged! Things were going well for me.

She looked fabulous in her tights and a long sweater. The sweater curved perfectly over her breasts and I tried hard not to stare. I looked at her legs, and even in those tights, they looked awesome. I wondered what it would be like to run my trembling hands over them; I sweated. She was irritatingly hot.

My respect for Arnab multiplied as I walked with Sarah
into that movie hall. He had kissed Sarah and done *stuff* while
I was shaking, and trembling and holding on to railings for
support. I also hated him a little. We we were shown our seats
by the usher. The movie had already started; it was a movie
starring Saif Ali Khan and Vidya Balan, and it was based on
a Bengali novel: *Parineeta*.

Slowly, we started talking about the movie; the proximity
of her body bothered me.

Ain't Vidya Balan fat?
Oh, that's a Bengali song.
She looks good.
Almost as good as you.
Thank you.

The innocuous truncated little dialogues went on for a
while. Muffled snickers. Laughs. A few stolen glances. Things
were going fine up until . . . they started becoming great. Slowly
and steadily, we had leaned into each other and our shoulders
touched; I wondered if it was intentional. Every time she
spoke or I did, our lips were hardly a few centimetres apart. I
breathed heavily and my heart pounded with nervous energy
every time the inches between us decreased.

I don't know what exactly happened, or how it did, but just
like that, she leaned over to say something and *stopped* . . . I
found myself staring at her lipstick-stained lips. Barely inches
away, her breath heavy on mine, the words that came out of
her mouth were slowly reduced to mumbles and her lips came
nearer till they hovered close to mine and quivered, and then
my lips brushed against hers, the wetness of hers on mine and
I enveloped her lips within mine as I always imagined I would,

and felt them one at a time. They were like marshmallows, never-ending soft, sweet marshmallows.

Soon, our tongues played with each other's. My hands were wrapped around her head and her fingers were in my hair. Slowly my hands slipped onto her neck and around her ears and she started writhing and moaning softly. My hands slipped further down onto her sweater, the moans got louder, she grabbed and clawed at my thigh, and we totally made out.

I hadn't even known how to kiss . . . or do anything else . . . before this, but everything just happened and it felt incredible. She must have done it a zillion times before, but I hadn't, so my smile was a gazillion times wider than hers was, and I didn't care. A little later, the usher spotted us and stood right near our seats, and we sunk into our seats, smiling, and we watched the rest of the movie without uttering a word. There was a constant grin on my face. Without a doubt, this was love, nothing else can feel so good.

The movie ended and we walked out of the theatre, her hand in mine. I wasn't the same Joy that had walked into the theatre. There was a voice inside me which was screaming, YOU JUST KISSED A GIRL! YOU'RE AWESOME! I think I even pumped my fist in happiness.

We spent a little time at a coffee shop nearby and we said we loved each other and that we missed each other. No more flapping tongues. No more hyperventilating. No more elevated heartbeats. No more stammering. That was the day I had shed the garb of being clueless in front of women; it was a turning point. I went back home with my head held high and a spring in my step. I was *awesome*. YES!

It took me quite some time to realize and accept why Sarah was with me—I reminded her of Arnab. I talked like him, I dressed like him and even my mannerisms were a reflection of his. He, unwittingly, had taught me how to talk, walk and do everything that worked to be with the times. I had picked up many things, intentionally or unintentionally, from him. Including his ex-girlfriend, my *first* love.

Over the next two months, we met quite a few times, mostly in movie halls, usually at odd times, to make sure that we were alone. It worked for her, too, for she never wanted anyone to know that we were going out. Years older and a lot wiser, I now understand that a rebound should always be kept under wraps. She didn't want anyone to know about *us*. I don't blame her for that, I was a step down from her earlier boyfriend, Arnab.

In the third month of our relationship, I told Arnab that I was seeing Sarah and that we, too, had done *stuff*. I also told him that I knew what all he had done with her. He was cool at first, but slowly, he lost it.

Shocked and enraged, he called Sarah up, and he shouted and bawled and called us traitors and man-sluts and whores.

Ex-boyfriends never let go of their ex-girlfriends. That's the lesson I learnt that day when Sarah called me up and dumped me. I cried myself to sleep for a few days, and then I told myself—there is *someone* else waiting, someone who doesn't have a sore ex-boyfriend. I slept on the bathroom floor for a few days because my stomach would churn and I would puke every time I thought of Arnab and Sarah together; my mother thought I had food poisioning and I had to take pills for that for an entire week. I had problems sleeping and I would clutch my pillow imagining it to be Sarah.

But despite my unending misery and the trauma, it was easier than I had thought it would be. In our short relationship, I used to think I would choke on my own tears and die if she were ever to leave me, but that clearly didn't happen, and that's because I knew she didn't love me for me—she loved me because she saw someone else in me. Though I did feel small and insignificant for months after the break-up—girls can make you feel like that.

And yes, I never saw Arnab again for a very long time. But over the years, I have thanked him in my head many times. For the confidence he built up in me . . . yes it was false and rooted in lies to begin with but fake it till you make it, right? I thank him for believing in me and for . . . Sarah. The girl in the short skirt and streaked hair.

***

'You guys are sick. Why would you ever discuss what you did with your girlfriends? You know that's just wrong, don't you?' I said.

'You wanted to hear it. I wasn't dying to tell you this,' Joy said.

'But streaked hair?'

'That used to be the in-thing back then, Neeti!' he said.

'By the way—Arnab? Who is that? The short, fat, bald person in your Facebook profile? Don't tell me he was your godfather. He is such a geek! Such a nerd,' I said.

Joy and I had been friends for a long time now. I knew every friend of his. And though he tried hiding who the real 'Arnab' was, I was sure my guess was bang on!

'Could be. Maybe. You never know. And by the way, the guy you are talking about is insanely rich and successful. . .'

'Whatever. I think I know who he is, and I still can't believe you looked up to him. He's so fat now! Anyway, you never saw Sarah again?'

'Not for a long time.'

'Never tried?' I asked. 'After all, first phone call, first girlfriend, first kiss . . . you shared a lot with her.'

'I did try, but not earnestly. I think she started dating someone else,' he said.

'Hmmm . . .' I smiled. I knew I had my man. Yes! 'What next?

Who was the next? Oh, you never told if you and Sarah, you know, like, DID it?'

'Nope, we never slept together. We just made out a few times and that's it. I was scared,' he said, almost embarrassed.

'So who was the unlucky girl who had to endure you?'

'My first true love,' he said and clicked on the folder named Sheeny.

'So did the two of you . . .?' I asked, not wanting to say it. And he nodded and smiled.

The folder opened.

Beautiful pictures. School dress. Beautiful hair. Kohl-lined eyes. Fair as snow. Sweet as hell.

'She lived in my colony and she was the sweetheart of all the roadside ruffians, she was the reason why guys came out in the evening . . . She was the beacon of innocence and cuteness, and she loved me for me,' Joy said.

'Wait, wait,' I said, looking at her pictures. 'Does she have light brown eyes? They are so pretty!'

'I know,' Joy said. 'The prettiest I have ever seen, and with her brown short hair that was always in a mess on her head like a mop, she could have passed off as a European. I used to spend hours looking at her,' he sighed, 'and her pictures,' he added.

And Joy started narrating again, and blinked away his tears.

The First Pill—Part 1

This was the time that Orkut had first made its presence felt, with its alluring scrapbooks, the communities, and the option to see who visited your profile last; it sounds ancient now, but it was a rage. *Everyone* had a profile! Within days, I too had a profile up there. I felt confident after my Sarah experience and so I started adding girls to my profile, left, right and centre. Anyone with a good profile picture worked.

Things were different back then. Since people were yet to realize that these social networking sites could be hunting grounds for perverts, people accepted random requests if they found the person interesting. Or good-looking.

My profile on Orkut was better than most people around, for I had joined the right communities, I put up pictures of the stacks of books I used to read, I tried to be witty in my scrapbook, and I wrote a very sensible 'About me'; my picture was adequately photoshopped; I had just one good picture where my hair was long and flopped over my forehead, and I had a patch of beard on my skin, somehow it all came together. I looked like an okay-looking, well-read, non-creepy guy from a premier engineering college.

A few days later, my mom came up to me and asked if I had put my name on the Internet somewhere.

'It's Orkut,' I said. 'It's a social networking site. Friends add each other, we can talk and drop scraps on their walls and tell them we like each other's pictures.' It sounded stupid.

'But all of you have phones!' she said. 'I don't know what you kids are up to these days on the Internet. Anyway, did you add Sheeny?'

I recalled that name in an instant. *Sheeny*. The neighbourhood sweetheart. If teenage guys were to decide real estate prices, our neighbourhood would be one of the most expensive localities to live in.

'Yes? *Why?*' I asked, nervously.

'Sheeny told her mom that you study in DCE and they were looking for a Physics teacher, so her mom asked—'

'Yes. I will teach her!' I said, before she could finish her sentence. My mom looked at me strangely, told me that she would tell Sheeny's mom, and left the room.

A week later, I was at Sheeny's home trying to teach her Electrostatics, and I was having trouble concentrating. She had the most incredible body for a seventeen-year-old; it was cute and cuddly, yet very attractive. At certain levels, she reminded me of Sarah, only Sheeny was fairer, shorter and cuter. A *lot* cuter. Her dimpled smile and charming demeanour was infectious, her messy brown hair, a thousand shades of brown, looked just perfect on her. I-don't-care-how-my-hair-looks-like hair.

It was not the first time I was seeing her, but I had never looked at her up close; I could hear my neighbourhood friends shouting and howling outside the window. The word had spread that I was to teach her.

'Why did you add me?' she asked as she chewed on her chewing gum. She flicked her hair off her face and looked at me.

'I remembered you from the community park function,' I lied. I knew her from *long* back.

Lies had started coming naturally to me. One relationship and you know the ground rules. *Lie if you want to live peacefully.*

'I never go to any of those.'

'You don't? I must have, like, found you in one of my friends' list and recognized you,' I said and she smiled. 'Why did you want me to teach you?'

'If I don't get into DCE or a good college through IP University, my parents will take me to Bangalore with them. And I don't want to go. I have friends here and I don't want to make new ones. The only good part about Bangalore is the men! They are so tan! I don't like fair guys, I am a bit of a racist,' she said, as she sat cross-legged on the bed in her tiny green hot pants and a yellow T-shirt two sizes too big—the transparent bra strap peeked out on her shoulder and it was very distracting. She was a riot of colours, and contrasts. A million shades in her hair, light brown eyes, yellow and green clothes, and the colourless strap. *Cute!*

'But why would you want me to teach you?'

'You are *cute*. And you are in DCE! That's even cooler. My friends will be so jealous,' she said and winked at me. She clutched tufts of her hair in both hands and pushed them away. Her eyes were beautiful, so brown.

'Your friends?' I asked, puzzled.

'All my friends have boyfriends, and I don't. And since they don't know you, I can tell them that I am seeing you!' she said, as casually as anyone could, still texting on her phone.

'Seeing me?' I asked, confused.

'Oh! I am sorry. I hope it will not be any trouble for you. And they hardly know you. So, it will be fine, I guess . . .' she said and placed her hand on mine. Obviously, it was okay. It would have been okay even if she told the whole world about it.

'You are kidding me!' I exclaimed and interrupted Joy .

'I had the same reaction,' Joy said. 'I asked her again, "Why me?" and she told me that I was cute and tanned! It was hard for me to believe someone could actually like the way I look. It was crazy! I went back home and looked at my reflection in the mirror for hours. I still felt I was ugly as hell!'

'And she is so pretty . . .' I said and flicked through some more pictures. 'How come she was single? And how on earth did she find you good-looking? Beats me.'

'Yes, it was strange,' he said. 'But isn't it always like that? The extremely pretty girls are always single. Like you,' he nudged me naughtily.

'Aww! Asshole,' I said. 'Anyway, continue.'

Joy closed the folder and continued with the story, 'Weeks passed and we were still to do a single question of physics. I had started to really enjoy her company and vice versa. The entire time, I couldn't tear my eyes off her.'

***

The First Pill—Part 2

'You have no intention of studying, do you?' I asked her as she sat on the computer, poring over someone's Orkut profile.

'Not really,' she said, blowing up her chewing gum till it burst all over her face. She was addicted to chewing gum, and I never found her not chewing one. The first drawer of her study table had all flavours of chewing gums from Wrigley's to Big Babool to Center Fresh; she was quite a chewing gum gourmet.

'I always wanted to know, Sheeny. How come *you* are single?'

'Umm . . . I don't know. The good guys never come up to me,' she said, switched off the computer and turned towards me. 'And now that you're my boyfriend, even the bad ones don't. I don't mind it much though. It's only when all my friends start to talk about their boyfriends and the sweet things they do for them, I feel left out.'

'Maybe you were always too good for the good guys. Maybe they think they don't have a shot at you.'

'Aww, you think so?'

'Most certainly,' I said. 'You are cute and you're smart!'

'Thank you,' she said, touching my arm again. 'You are just being sweet!'

'No. I am serious. I would have never thought that I had a chance with you. *Really*. It would be awesome if I were dating you for real!'

I regretted those words as soon as they left my mouth; she stopped chewing and looked at me, and I was about to apologize but she came and sat next to me, and said, 'For *real*?'

'Yes,' I responded, trembling.

'That would be cool. I, anyway, really like you,' she said, blushing. 'And you are a nice guy, fun to be with, and you are kind of hot. You're not too tall either!'

My face felt warm, I was blushing. She came closer. I repeated the sentence in my head again. Nobody had called me *hot* before! There has to be some mistake.

'Thank you. And you are pretty awesome, too. So . . .' I said, not knowing what to say.

'So?' she asked, her eyes big and expectant, like a little schoolgirl from those Manga comics.

'Will you go out with me? Like for real?' I said, sweat on my brow, panicking; I felt the walls close in on me. 'Umm, be my girlfriend? A real girlfriend? Not just to tell your friends?'

'I expected you to say something better,' she chuckled, 'but this will do! *Yes*!'

She hugged me and a huge smile broke out on her face. 'You looked so adorable when you said that!'

Then just like that, she kissed me on the cheek. Instantly, small bolts of electricity ran through my body. I felt a tingling sensation running through my fingers and toes. She held me with her hands around my neck.

'And you always look adorable,' I said and kissed her back on the forehead. Once. Twice. Thrice. We stared into each other's eyes, our breathing completely coordinated, heavy and expectant. I knew what was going to happen next, but the voice inside me was screaming aloud, 'IMPOSSIBLE! YOU'RE A HIDEOUS BOY AND SHE'S AN AMAZING GIRL!'

She looked into my eyes and then lowered them to my lips. Mine followed the same trajectory, inching towards hers until we kissed, softly. She retreated a little and then came closer, looked at me and smiled. This time, *she* inched forward and kissed *me*. She tasted very fruity, I guessed from the chewing gum but I didn't ask. I spent the rest of the evening giggling like a little girl, and I told her about the far-reaching fame of her enviable looks. We talked in hushed tones and kept an eye on her mother who was cooking all this while in the kitchen.

Our classes soon went from holding hands, to telling each other about our school and colleges, to talking about our crushes (and she had many!), to stealing kisses whenever we could, and then one day when her mother was visiting my house, we found ourselves considerably naked and wrapped around each other, our legs intertwined in an inseparable and awkward maze. We were exhausted. I don't think I was very good at making out, but it surely felt unlike anything I have ever felt before.

'Joy?' she said, as she looked at me with her wide-open eyes. 'How many girls have you kissed before me?'

'Is that important?'

'To me, it is,' she said, as she looked away and rested her head on my shoulder.

'Just one. And I didn't like her as much,' I said, as I kissed her forehead.

'Really?' she looked at me.

'Yes,' I said.

'You are my first guy,' she said and smiled at me. Her smile, I still maintain, was the best sight in the world. 'And I wish you to be my last, Joy.'

After that day, we went for three weeks without kissing or holding hands, or even having a proper conversation without someone interrupting us. Her cousins were in Delhi from Bangalore and we always had company, often little baby brothers, irritating as hell and not cute at all. She tried meeting me outside the house a few times but a cousin would always accompany her. It made her restless, it made me lose my mind; I wanted her so bad!

A day before they left, Sheeny had texted me that her folks would be at the airport the next day and that I should get protection, and god knows, I read the text about four million times. I intended to text her back the question, *WHY?*, but I thought it would be pretty stupid; the sentence was self-explanatory and all-encompassing. How I got the protection is a long and embarrassing story in itself, and I should save it for some other time.

I went online and searched forums for Tips & Tricks for first-timers. Everyone seemed to say, *just go with the flow*, as if that made any sense at all! Listless, I called up Sidharth, who is a bit of know-it-all and the only guy I can discuss this with. Sidharth became kind of like my best friend after Arnab and I fell apart. In fact, he almost became my girlfriend for we talked for hours every day, yakking about girls, careers, professors, his crazy ideologies about life in general, and hung out together, often to the horror of my parents, especially since it was around this time that people started talking about gay rights with alarming frequency.

Anyway, Sidharth had always been the go-to guy. Problem-solver. Tall. Good-looking. With the craziest of ideas. Very straightforward. His father worked in the stock market and his cash flows depended on how the stock market behaved each week.

'You are a lucky bastard!' Sidharth said. 'I mean, I have this cousin in the eleventh grade and he is in a band and everything, so you know, he is at the top of the social pyramid. He says that though almost everyone has a girlfriend now, only some of them make out and stuff. And sex is still pretty uncommon. So your girlfriend is a nymphomaniac!'

'Fuck off, Sidharth! She's my girlfriend. Watch it! She is very sweet and I love her!' I said, defending her; I was uncharacteristically angry. After all, she was my first legitimate girlfriend.

'Sweet? She asks you to fuck her so soon and she is sweet? Bullshit! She just wants it,' Sidharth said.

'She *loves* me.'

'Whatever. I think you should act on it before she changes her mind. You know how girls are, right?'

I realized soon that even Sidharth couldn't help me out in this matter, and we soon disconnected the call.

Despite all my preparations and heavy Googling, we didn't do it the next time, or the time after that, and the time after that. I wasn't *ready*. I just freaked out every time and so did she; this was much more difficult than kissing and bad make-out sessions. We were both not ready. At least, I wasn't. I felt like a gigantic loser, and I wondered if there was a bigger douchebag than I was. Every time we tried, I would go back home cursing myself, thinking about Sheeny and how I disappointed her, and wondering about how the wearing protection part fits into the whole sex thing. It's mechanical, unromantic and downright impractical; I think I even started hating the thought of making love.

Eventually we stopped talking about it, and things crawled back to normal. It was a Monday, and I don't know why I remember the day because I am bad at days, but I remember that she had just come out of the shower. Her hair was wet and she looked inviting. The room was redolent with the fragrance of her face wash and her shampoo and her body wash. I was drawn to her, and I kissed her. Twenty minutes later, we were spent. We had *done* it. Finally. Surprisingly, I felt more relieved than happy (but it was also fantastic!) and I realized I really didn't hate the thought of making love as much. The hype, the wait, the anticipation—all of it had lived up to the expectations. The sheer pleasure of having her body next to me, writhing and struggling in pain and ecstasy was unmatchable. Like they say, I will never forget my first time. But, as they say, every rose has its thorn. The pleasure was short-lived. Soon, tension was in the air and it engulfed us.

She had bled, but that was the least of our problems. Somewhere in the act, I had heard, and felt a *snapping* sound, and so had she. But we were so busy moaning out loud, digging our claws into each other and groaning periodically, that we had chosen to ignore it. The sound was of the protection snapping; it had torn.

'It's the first time this has happened,' I said, not wanting any part of the blame on my ignorance. Maybe I had just put it on wrong. 'We shouldn't have done it! Damn it!'

'Shit. Are you sure . . . you know?' she said as the worry lines on her head became prominent; this was nightmarish. I nodded.

We immediately started counting dates from her last

period. I had read somewhere on the forums about the *dates* when having sex would be most safe. Anyway, I let her do the counting and she didn't seem too happy about it.

'It's not even one of those fucking safe dates,' she said and held her head in her hands. She had started crying a little. 'A girl in Modern School even got pregnant . . . her parents . . .'

'Nothing like that will happen,' I said. 'Let me check on the Internet.'

'I will go take a bath,' she said and rushed to the washroom, wailing.

I typed in the Google search bar: *Condom burst. What next? Condom Burst. Pregnancy? Pregnancy test.*

I Googled everything.

Emergency Contraceptives.

This word stood out. I Googled again.

Emergency Contraceptives India

Darn!

In India, these were still prescription drugs whereas in the US, they were sold over-the-counter. No wonder, India is bursting with people. One condom snaps, and you have a kid in your hands, and your parents disown you and you have to marry the guy! I waited as she took quite some time in the washroom. I pinned my ears to the door and could hear her cry inside. I didn't know what to say.

'We need to see a doctor,' I said, as I tried to stay calm, but I was freaking out.

'What?'

'Pills,' I said.

'I am not taking them . . . They are not good for the body . . . they do something to your cycles and . . . Joy, what if Mom . . . or Dad . . . I can't do this . . .' she said. She looked tense. She still hadn't stopped crying, and I wasn't helping.

'But we can't just sit and do nothing. We have to do it!'
I said.

'It's easier for you to say. I will ask my friends.'

'What do they know? I just Googled. It's all safe. It's even sold over-the-counter in the US.'

'Just leave,' she said, still crying.

'But . . . Let's at least talk to a doctor . . .'

'*Joy*. Just *leave*!' she shouted.

Throughout the next day, I kept calling her and texting her, persuading her to come with me to see a doctor. Time was running out and I was losing my head. *Seventy-two hours*, I had read on the Internet; there wasn't much time left. I cursed her for being so irresponsible and thinking only about herself; I called her selfish and reckless. She just cried, listened, disconnected the call and switched off her phone. The following night, after I had gone to sleep, my phone beeped. It was from Sheeny. The message read.

Taken the pill. Went with a friend. Don't worry. Take Care.

Women. They are strange, aren't they?

The thought of taking her to a doctor had made me wet my pants, even though I was the guy. She was younger, yet bolder and stronger. This is why such things are always left to women. The more important things in life. Men just aren't up to the task. At least *I* wasn't. I really didn't know why she wouldn't go there with me. She did end up taking the pill after all.

***

'Maybe she just wanted a little support from you before you started giving her options, Joy. She was looking at you to make her stop crying and not Google and give her options straightaway!' I said.

'Why didn't she just tell me so?' Joy protested.

'She was just a kid, Joy. She wanted you to hug her and tell her that it would be okay.'

'But I said that!'

'You told her to take a pill!'

'But that's what . . . that would have solved everything,' he said.

All men are the same and Joy was no different. They think only they can come up with solutions, but what they don't understand is, we don't want solutions . . . we want support and care and love.

'Whatever. But she did love you, didn't she?' I asked Joy.

Joy paused for a while before he said, 'Yes, she did.'

'Then what happened? Why did you guys break up?'

'You have to understand here that I didn't know what loving someone meant. This was my first real relationship and she was an incredible girl. I didn't know whether I just wanted to be with her or that I was in love with her . . . All I knew was that any guy would be in love with a girl like her. I cared about her, but . . .'

***

41

The First Pill—Part 3

Sheeny and I completed three months. The whole contraceptive episode was behind us primarily because she didn't want to talk about it. We were still making love (and it was unreal!) whenever her mother wasn't around, and we took care she didn't have to take a pill again.

Though the relationship was nothing extraordinary—and I know it's a terrible thing to say—but that was how it was. If I think about it, it went on because neither one of us had been in a real relationship before to know what to expect out of it. She was pretty and smart and funny, but we would run out of things to talk about. We would spend hours on the phone, and only she would talk, about her friends, about the homework she couldn't complete, about the teacher who was constantly after her life, the boys of her school who would constantly flirt with her, and I would listen to her talk, not because it interested me, but because that's what good boyfriends do. I always felt that I had been insanely lucky to be with someone as incredible as Sheeny, and it led me to believe that I should have no reasons to complain.

Sheeny often told me that I was good-looking, something

that I found ridiculous, but I never complained; she was good for my ego. I had every reason to stay in the relationship. It felt *great* to be seen with her.

Despite everything good in the relationship, the spark in the relationship was dying out, and it wasn't as if were fighting, but we just didn't have ANYTHING to talk about. We were still into each other, groping, kissing and biting whenever we had a chance (because, well, I am a guy), but that was the only real motive I had left to meet her. Other than that, our dates were really *monotonous*.

'The pasta is great, isn't it?' she asked. 'You know what? The girl in my class whose boyfriend went to the army? He is getting married now and he didn't even bother to tell this girl. Isn't that so unfair? I mean, what harm would it have done to that guy if he had just told her beforehand . . . it's silly, isn't it?'

'Yes,' I said, as I continued eating.

'You seem a little off today. What's the problem?' Sheeny asked.

How could I have told her that I wasn't interested in her stories about her girlfriends? It was either that or how a cute boy in her class approached her. I always wondered why she never noticed that I wasn't interested in her stories. I know now that she might have, but she was in love with me; just the thought of someone being in love with me was ridiculous.

'No, I am just a little tired,' I said.

'Okay . . . then just listen. My parents went to our old house in Patparganj yesterday and found that . . .' she resumed her stories and I resumed eating.

Things kept getting *worse*. I couldn't talk in the same language or couldn't take part in the conversations she wanted to have. It was strange because just a few months back, I would have killed to get her to talk to me, but things had changed.

There were times when I just didn't want to be with her. I preferred being alone. But then again, she was cute and *good* in bed and I was still a nerd, unloved by anyone else, and that's what made it very hard to stay away from her.

~

'What?' Sidharth said. '*Break up with her?* Are you crazy? You know how many guys ask me every day about the girl you are dating? And you do realize that you wouldn't find someone as hot as her. *Ever.* You're like the monkey in *King Kong* holding the pretty girl!'

'It was the gorilla.'

'Yes, you're the gorilla.'

'Thank you for taking my side,' I say. 'I know. But, I feel bored now,' I had started to sound like Arnab.

'*Bored*? Only rich good-looking guys have the right to say that. When a girl like Sheeny dates someone as average and un-extraordinary as you, you just suck it all up and date and be with her, come what may!'

'C'mon, Sidharth. We have nothing to talk about! All we do is sit in the front of the television and watch movies. We have nothing in common. I am not even sure I love her. Shouldn't she know that?'

'When exactly did you have a sex change? Shut up with all the honesty! Feel lucky that you're not in love. Being in love is painful, man,' Sidharth sighed.

Yeah, he was in love with Vani, tall, beautiful and very feminine. I didn't think their relationship would last, but it did and it had been six months now.

He continued, '. . . I see her with other guys, I blow my top. If I don't talk to her, I don't feel like doing anything else.

If hours go by without any news of her, I freak out. Being in love is *terrible* man. I would love to be where you are. I'm still a goddamn virgin!'

'I would trade places with you any day.'

'Because you're a girl in a man's body. Like, seriously, you don't deserve your balls,' Sidharth concluded.

Hypocrite.

'I'm just scared, man. She falls more in love each day and it freaks me out. The later I break up, the more she is going to cry. And I don't want that to happen.'

Sidharth didn't get it. After a while, I stopped trying to explain it to him, and we talked about Sachin Tendulkar instead.

~

'They said it was okay if I stayed in Delhi!' Sheeny said with moist eyes and her voice cracking.

Both of us knew she was never going to make it to any engineering college in Delhi. But she had told her parents that in any case, she wouldn't go to Bangalore with them. Her parents were strictly against it, but she had been firm in her stand. Fortunately, or *unfortunately*, she had succeeded.

'That's wonderful!' I said, faking my enthusiasm.

'Isn't that great? All I have to do is try to get into some decent Delhi University course . . . I don't think I am anyway good enough for any of the engineering colleges.'

'Don't say that,' I said and hugged her. She was undoubtedly extremely happy that day. She held my hand throughout the day and kissed me at every opportunity. *I felt burdened.*

Somewhere deep inside my heart, I wanted her to *go*. It would have made things so much easier for me. I had never dumped anyone and I saw no reason why I should dump her. It was *unfair*. She was so sweet to me, loved me like anything and she was beautiful. She didn't deserve to get dumped. And most importantly, *I didn't know how to dump someone!* Anyway, her happiness was short-lived as her parents changed their mind the next day. That day she came crying to me for *support*.

'You fought again?' I asked.

'Yes. I don't know why they don't get it. I *want* to stay here. I don't want to go there. I never wanted to. They should get it. It's my life, it's my decision.'

'Sheeny, they should, but you are their only daughter and you are very pretty. They obviously feel worried about you. You can't be so rude to them. At least don't *fight*,' I said.

I knew what I was doing there—*brainwashing her*. Every fibre of my being cursed me for doing what I was, but it was infinitely better than telling her that I didn't love her, that I never had, and that I was with her because I had no reason not to be with her.

'*They* don't get it. I have tried every possible thing. I wish I could just tell them that it's because of *you* I want to stay here so much.'

'Don't ever say that to them,' I said, wondering what her mom would say to mine, '. . . it would be so unfair to your parents. You know them for the last eighteen years; you can't just leave them for someone you have met just a few months back.'

'Ummm,' she said. 'Do you want me stay, Joy?'

'What kind of question is that?'

'It's as simple as questions get,' she said with a straight face. 'Do you want me to stay?'

'Obviously, I want you to stay,' I said.

'I wonder why you never say that,' she said and looked away, her eyes still moist.

This was the first conversation of many, where I mildly hinted to her that she shouldn't go against her parents, and that she needed to respect their wishes. Maybe, this was the time I had changed into a guy who started disregarding the feelings of people around me. Especially of those who dated me.

Anyhow, another two months of many such conversations, bad results in examinations and the fact that I kept assuring her that long-distance relationships work, made her bow down to her parents' wishes. She was going to Bangalore. I felt relieved, and I hated myself with a vengeance. It was totally *her* decision, but it was taken by *me*. I burdened her with so much guilt about fighting with her parents that she just had to go.

Mom had asked me to drive them to the airport, and I did so.

'So this is it . . .' she said. 'Bye, Joy,' she hugged me as her parents walked away from us and towards the airport terminal.

'Keep calling. Take a number as soon as you get there and give me a call,' I said.

'Joy . . .' she said.

'Yes?'

'I am not going to do that,' she said.

'What? Wha . . . what are you *not* going to do?'

'I am not going to call you. We will not be in contact. This is it,' she said, almost dispassionately. 'This is the end of the road for us.'

'What are you saying? Are you all right? Why would you not call me?' I asked.

Now that she had said it, it felt kind of terrible that she would never call again. I was almost in tears, my stomach churned.

'Yes, I am good, Joy. Had you wanted me around, you would have tried to keep me around. Instead you . . . pushed me away.' Tears now rolled down her cheeks even as she said that.

'I didn't! I *love* you. I want you around. I have always wanted you around!'

Now, I panicked. The crushing emptiness of my life that would engulf me after she left hit me then. No calls from her would be disastrous. If not anything else, I was used to her now. She was a part of my life, a beautiful part of my life.

'No you don't. Have a good life. Love you,' she said and kissed my forehead. 'I will always think of you . . . You will *always* be special . . .' she said and shook my hand, passing on a note to me.

And she walked away. I saw her disappear behind the doors. She never looked back.

I read the note:

Is it a tear for the kiss we had,
or a tear for the love that left,
is it a tear for those fights over milkshakes,
or a tear for this ugly heartbreak,
is it a tear for I thought you were the one,
or a tear for by my side there is none,
I understand it didn't go well,
those trees couldn't hold our name for long,
I understand that kiss under the stars,
has lost its magic and its charm,
I understand that all I sought for,
is now shattered to pieces like a glass,
and so now I have to take it in my face,
and we'll have to walk apart!
I understand how much I want to stay . . .

But now I'll have to walk away.

I felt my heart sink.

But isn't that what I wanted? For her to go away? But then, why did I start missing her almost immediately? I felt like a shitty person, I missed the person I used to be, the shy person who used to measure his words before saying them, and the introvert who never talked to people and hurt them.

Between that day and now, I have tried to search for her on Orkut, Facebook, and other social networking sites and have found her nowhere.

Sheeny Sharma, Bangalore, 9 April 1988. None of the searches gave anything. I know *why* those searches don't work.

I wish I could see her once and tell her how sorry I am. And I wish she is happy *wherever* she is. And that she thinks about me occasionally.

***

'You almost sound as if you still miss her, Joy,' I said. Joy had narrated the last part with glazed eyes and a quivering voice.

'I do,' he said. 'You never really forget your first relationship . . . and . . . and . . . I feel guilty about what I did to her . . . and how she left. I just wish I could see her once . . . Just once. If not anything else, just to tell her that I am sorry.'

'What crap! You never feel guilty about dumping someone!' I said. It was strange to hear such a thing out loud, in the open . . .

'Things were different then, I miss her. I miss her every day.'

'So Sheeny is the mystery woman whom you never met after you lost your virginity to her,' I said. 'Now that's a better story.' I smiled.

'Hmmm,' he said, his eyes were wet, and he looked away. He looked strangely upset. I had rarely seen him this upset before. I didn't know anything about this girl so I was a little surprised. I didn't want to intrude but I couldn't help but ask him as to what was wrong.

'What happened?' I asked. 'You seem pretty upset.'

'I should have never let her go,' Joy said, his voice breaking and trailing off.

'That's sweet,' I said.

And suddenly, the tears at the corners of his eyes rolled down.

He did not attempt to make them stop. He mumbled and whispered to himself. I didn't hear it the first time he said it. 'I killed her . . .' he whispered.

'What?' I said, shocked, not believing what I had just heard.

'Two days after she landed in Bangalore . . . she died.'

'What are you saying, Joy?'

With tears in his eyes, guilt crushing his heart, he told me that he had contacted a friend of Sheeny's a few days after she had left. She told him that Sheeny had passed away in a car crash, days after she landed in Bangalore.

'Her friend blamed me for it,' Joy said.

'C'mon.'

I didn't know what to say. What can anyone say at such a time? I just wished he would stop crying.

'She was right. Had I not let her go . . . she would still be alive.'

'Joy, no one can predict these things,' I said. 'It wasn't your fault!'

'All she needed was a little love from me. I just had to ask her once to stay back. I couldn't even do that.'

'It's not your fault, Joy.'

'It's my fault, Neeti. I am just a very selfish person.'

'No, you're not.'

'I could have saved her,' he said and buried his face in his palms. I sat next to him and hugged him. It was strange to see a guy who was always smiling, cry so much. I had nothing to say. I could see the guilt in Joy's eyes. He looked terrible and said he truly believed he caused whatever had happened to her. I assured him otherwise and tried to change the topic. But he couldn't get over it.

'It is okay, Joy,' I said again, as he kept breaking down.

'I saw the mangled car on the Internet . . . just to imagine that she was in there,' his voice trailed off.

'Joy . . .'

'She was in the car because of me . . .'

'It's not your fault, Joy!'

Joy repeated the same sentences over and over and I felt sorry for him. After a while and numerous attempts, I was finally successful in changing the topic. It took me an hour to do that, but I was glad he had stopped crying.

'Anyway, tell me a little about Sidharth . . . I know all your friends, but I still haven't figured out who he is,' I said.

'Okay. There was an incident involving him. And the first time ever I saw how people react when cheated on . . .'

'Go on,' I said, although I really had no interest in that story. But as far it distracted him from thinking about Sheeny, it was fine for me.

'Fine,' he said, and sipped on the remnants of the coffee in his cup. 'He was madly in love with Vani.'

He wiped away the dried streaks of his tears and started to narrate.

The First Cheating—Part 1

After Sheeny went away, a long lull descended. It was not that I craved to be with anyone but it was hard to get Sheeny out of my head. The guilt had crushed me. I was more in *love* with her after she went away than when she was around. I used to spend days locked in my room, listening to the songs we had heard together, remembering the times I used to stare at her in disbelief that she was actually dating me, and I really really missed her.

'You don't know what you've got till it's gone . . . They paved paradise, put up a parking lot.'

I spent months reeling under the impact of what had happened. The conversation that I had with Sheeny's friend kept playing on repeat in my head, every day, throughout the day. The pictures from the net, of the mangled car and blood, kept flashing in front of me. I kept blaming myself for having led her to her fate. Not a single day passed without my reading the note she had slipped into my hand when she shook it . . . for the *last* time.

I am sorry. If only I could just say these words to her now.

I stopped seeing anyone. I failed in a couple of subjects in college and my attendance dipped, but no matter how hard I tried, I just couldn't get her, or what I had done to her, out of my head. Sidharth tried to make it better, but with my constant snubs and depressing demeanour, he, too, gave up. Mom and Dad were worried and they often wondered if I needed to be taken to a doctor. Everybody knew what had happened and Mom had started assuring me that it wasn't my fault. But *nothing* worked. The business of breaking up and losing someone is terrible.

But as it happens, time heals everything. Even though I was far from being okay, I got better with time.

'You need to go out, man!' Sidharth said for the tenth time that evening. Exams had just finished and I had insisted that we stay home. I still had a lot of grieving to do. This dying business is really horrendous.

'You have to get it out of your system. You can't stay and be like this all your life. What happened, has happened. You have to *move* on. Sheeny would have wanted you to move on . . .'

'Don't give me that crap. Dead people want nothing,' I said.

'Oh shut up. See, I will call up Vani and ask her to get a friend along. What say?'

'I don't know,' I said.

Obviously, such a reaction couldn't stand up to the constant egging on by Sidharth. Later that evening, we were speeding down the lanes of Delhi University to pick up Vani and her friend. Supposedly, her friend was hot, so I thought that maybe it wasn't that bad an idea after all. I *desperately* needed a time out.

'Hi,' she said. Sidharth and Vani had left on his bike for the metro station while they asked the two of us to get onto a rickshaw. It was a set-up and both of us knew it. I was still thinking of my dead girlfriend; she was way prettier. Why do we even talk of 'forever' when someone eventually has to die? John Green was right, 'All relationships either end in break-ups, divorce or death.' My relationship gets ticks on two out of three boxes.

'Hi. Joy,' I thrust out my hand.

'Srishti.'

'Nice name.'

'Same to you,' she said and we smiled.

She reminded me of someone faintly. It didn't take me long to guess who. Nisha. Short, fair, edible and chirpy. On a closer look, she wasn't. It was just that it had been so long since I had been with a girl alone that she looked kind of, border-line, attractive to me.

By the way, in all these months I had heard Nisha had started going out with someone. I had checked that guy out on Orkut and I have to admit, he looked like an asshole. *The Asshole Boyfriend Syndrome.*

Anyway, minutes later we were chatting about everything under the sun. Well, *she* was, and I was listening to her, wondering if my ears were bleeding. I decided I didn't like her at all. She talked too much. I wanted to stuff her mouth with my socks.

'You DCE guys have it good. You will get a good job after you pass out, a degree that will hold on for a lifetime, awesome to get into any of the good management colleges . . . Life's set, you know. For Zoology honours, things are little too difficult . . . We slog so much . . . and then we do our post-graduation, our PhD in shitty, ill-equipped labs for years on end, and then don't even get a job worth working for . . .'

'You can't blame yourself for it . . . there are just not enough medical seats in the country,' I said as I tried to sympathize with her.

The minute we got down from the rickshaw, we found Vani and Sidharth staring at us mischievously, as if we already had it going. Little did they know that by this time, my ears were numb. *Nightmare*. She had talked about Zoology, marriage, her childhood, love life, her plans—*everything!* I wanted to ask her to stop and breathe and have a glass of water.

I thanked God when we entered the movie theatre but it started again.

'The movie is so slow I can go home, eat, change, come back and it would still be at the place where it is,' Srishti said.

'Yes,' I said as I kept my sentences as short as possible so as to avoid any conversation.

'Will you guys *shut* up?' Vani whisper-screamed.

'Or go out of here if you want to talk!' Sidharth also whisper-screamed and winked at me.

'Let's go,' she said.

'What?' I said as I almost shat my pants.

'Let's go! Now!' she said and clutched my hand. I wished I had an axe to saw her hand off.

'Sure,' I said and we left the auditorium, and then the hall. Things were just perfect; I was so much better at home, sulking and crying.

'This is so much better,' she said as we entered the coffee shop nearby. We ordered our coffee. I ordered a huge sandwich and hoped she would eat more and talk less.

'At least we can talk here,' she said. I would have rather hung myself by my testicles.

'I know,' I said and took a sip. I knew she would start a conversation, as that had been the usual trend that afternoon. I looked for ear buds to shut her voice out.

'So . . . Sidharth told me that you had been crying all day since your break-up. I always thought that was something that we girls did.'

'Actually, she died,' I said.

'Oh, I am sorry,' she responded. She sipped on her coffee and stayed shut for a while, trying to process what I had just told her.

'What do you think of Sidharth?' she asks, breaking the soothing silence I had started to savour.

'He's a nice guy,' I answer.

'I like the guy. He loves his girl way too much. That's very rare. I always thought of him as being too much of a player to be so much in love, but he's very genuine.' And she went on and on and on . . . It went from annoying to downright irritating to *Shut-the-fuck-up-or-I-will-fucking-blow-your-head-off!*

She just went on, '. . . and when these two started going out, I just thought it was just a fling you know, like Vani going after the tall guys who look like they would be great in bed and stuff. It was all too quick and suddenly, Sidharth, after just a few months, told her that he wanted to be with her like for good, get married and all that. It *freaked* me out. Marry Sidharth? Now that was not something even Vani . . .'

'Wait? *What?* Sidharth proposed?' Now this was interesting. For the first time that evening, I didn't want to kill her; this was interesting gossip.

'You didn't know? Ohh! Anyway, even we were shocked. I mean I was. Vani just lost her mind. She was unbelievably happy! I mean, c'mon! They are just twenty! They couldn't be making plans about something six years down the line. Plus her thing with Aman, it was all too complicated to handle. I don't know what Vani was thinking.'

'*Aman?* Her ex-boyfriend? Wasn't that all in the past? What now?' I said, a little taken aback.

'I shouldn't tell you this but I think Vani still has feelings for that guy. And it's strange because after what he did with her, she should have just snapped all ties. Anyway, she still talks to him; I think she even met him a few days back. I don't know what the deal is with this girl. She is just so confused.'

I forgot about being angry at Srishti, now I was furious at Vani. I remember Sidharth telling me about Vani's ex-boyfriend, a gigantic jerk, and he told me that Vani and Aman don't talk anymore.

'Are you sure about it?' I asked.

'Yes. But don't tell Sidharth. In all probability, she will sort things out and tell him herself. But it's between the two of them and *we* shouldn't interfere or comment. I mean after all it's their life and their problem . . . who are *we* to comment on it!' she said.

You are the one who is commenting, bitch!

After this, I just stopped listening to whatever she had to say. I was battling thoughts of whether I would tell Sidharth or not. It took me a week to decide that I shouldn't do anything about it. And it took two weeks for Sidharth to know *all* about it.

***

'What is it with you guys?' I asked.

'As in?' Joy said.

'I mean, guys are always in touch with their ex-girlfriends, that's not a problem. But when we do, it is! Such double standards,' I protested.

'Oh, you are such a kid,' Joy said, disdainfully. 'Look. In a relationship, girls set examples. Guys follow. Girls are the good ones in a relationship. They teach the guys how to behave! Girls, in reality, are the better halves. They aren't allowed such liberties as talking to exes. Because it's a bad example! Especially since everyone knows that girls give everything to a relationship. And that's what we expect. And in that state of having lost your minds and hearts to us, if you are still in touch with your ex-boyfriend, it's just bad news. The male brain is hardwired to react violently to that.'

'You don't make sense,' I said, though in my heart of hearts, I did find some sense in what Joy had just said.

'Whatever,' he said. 'Should I continue?'

'Sure,' I said, still a little pissed off.

'Sidharth blew his top off. I knew his temper. He is not the type of person you should mess with,' Joy said.

This part, I listened to with extra interest. I knew now who the

59

real Sidharth was. I would be lying if I said I didn't like him. In fact, I had a huge crush on him back in the day. His smouldering hot, intense eyes always struck me. But Joy didn't want complications in his friendships and never introduced us formally.

I wish . . .

***

The First Cheating—Part 2

'**H**ow could she? *She lied, right to my face!*' Sidharth said with teary bloodshot eyes. It was almost a little strange to see a big man like him cry. '*Right to my fucking face!*'

'C'mon. Get over it. She didn't deserve you,' I said. The *usual* post-break-up dialogue; he looks at me as if he would break my face.

Vani never told Sidharth. Sidharth spotted the two of them together at a coffee shop near her house. When he confronted her, the guy said it was none of his business. They ended up having a big spat there, and Sidharth was left with a bruised hand, and the ex-boyfriend got his nose smashed.

As illogical as girls are, Sidharth was blamed for the whole episode, she called him *irresponsible* and that he should have tried talking it out. Sidharth told her that she was a *bitch* and should fuck every ex-boyfriend she had had. Quite obviously, she never wanted to see him again, and Sidharth asked her to go fuck herself, which contradicted his previous sentence.

'Let's call up Ganesh. Let's have a go at this guy. He fucked up and I am going to *fuck* his happiness up, man,' he said, pacing around the room.

Ganesh was a troublemaker, a friend of Sidharth's, who was always looking for people to beat up; it was like his profession and he pursued it passionately. We had seen the guys who had been at the receiving end of Ganesh's assaults and they were not pretty sights.

'Sleep it off. The fight is not going to help the situation. And I guess if someone is wrong, it's Vani.'

'I know, but I love her. And the fight will help. Anyway, it's *over* between her and me. At least this would make me feel a little better.'

'But . . .'

'We should deal with Aman. That *fucking* asshole. Teach him a fucking lesson that he wouldn't forget.' His voice cracked from anger and despair, as he clenched both his fists and banged them on the table. I was already scared.

'Shut up, man. Take it easy. Give it a few days, it will all be fine,' I said.

'It will not be fine, man. She fucked up and I have full right to have my revenge. I am not going to take this lying down. I mean I have to do something. What would *you* have done if your girl was doing the same?'

'I have never been in love,' I said, trying to joke, though I know I am someone who would never get into fights; I know I will just end up running.

'*Lucky* bastard,' he said.

'Okay.'

'But you have no idea, Joy, what I am going through right now. I can't sleep, I can't eat . . . I'm dying, man.'

'You're overreacting. Get *over* it!'

'It's not easy. All I do is think about these two talking, saying things to each other, even kissing, oh fuck, I am sure, kissing. *Ugh*. That slut! And that bastard,' he said, his face turning red.

'If you are so angry with *her*, why do this to the *guy*?'

'Because he is a motherfucking asshole. You don't know how he dumped Vani. He fucking made her *cry* for months! And who was with her all that time? It was *me*! And just when everything is perfect, this shit-eating *bastard* comes up and fucking spoils everything.'

'Hey, Sidharth. Calm down, man.'

'Calm down? Are you crazy?'

'Okay, you are right. I probably don't know what you are going through. But stay put. Don't do anything rash. Don't do anything at all. Things will be all right. Just give it a few days. They'll work out. If things don't get fine, I promise I will go with you when you bash him up. I promise.'

'Promise?' he asked me, tears of anger in his eyes.

'On my life! On our friendship,' I said, in earnest.

And nothing was fine. Sidharth spent three entire weeks locked up at his place, reminding me of the times I have done the same; we are pretty vulnerable boys it seems. He wasn't picking up anyone's calls, not even mine. His parents called me up to ask what had gone wrong and I gave them some lame excuse which they didn't buy; our parents are usually smarter than what we give them credit for. It was freaking me out. Sidharth was not the kind of guy who would be hung up over something for too long. Something *big* was going to happen this time, and I feared that, and I had to be a part of it, I had promised.

The fourth week, he showed up. He stood beneath my balconyand made roaring noises on the engine of his bike. I smelled trouble. He motioned me to get on the bike and refused to say anything as we sped across the streets of our neighbourhood. No words were exchanged. As we crossed the third signal, we were joined by three other bikes and a big car full of menacing, angry people. The road filled up with roars of engines and people shouting and cursing their lungs out. The guys in the car looked dangerous. I would have pissed my pants had I not been on the same side as them.

The ex-boyfriend's worst nightmare was to come true that day. We screeched to a halt outside a college. We waited.

I saw a big guy step down from the car; I dared not say anything, because I don't think I had seen such anger in anyone's eyes before. They were brimming with unbridled rage. *Ganesh*.

'Joy.'

'Hi, Ganesh,' I said. Even though he was on my side, I was still shitting in my pants, my eyes on the knuckle-buster he had already slipped his hand into.

'I heard you were stopping Sidharth from beating up the asshole,' he said, as he put his hand around me. He took a puff on the cigarette that dangled from the edge of his mouth and waited for an answer.

'I just thought, why get into all this trouble . . . you know,' I said.

'Ohh, that's where you got it wrong, beta. We are not getting into any trouble. The other guy is,' he laughed and the guys with him echoed the same laughter.

'So what do you plan to do with him?' I asked.

'Whatever he plans,' Ganesh smiled and pointed at Sidharth. The smile on Ganesh's face was really unpleasant, almost gruesome.

All this while, Sidharth didn't flinch; he wore a deadpan

expression, though his eyes were furious. He had not shaved in many days and looked sinister. He was focused on the man who was to come out from that college gate.

'That's *him*,' Sidharth said.

And then, I recognized the guy whom I had seen on Facebook. *Aman*, the poor ex-boyfriend—like a lamb walking to its slaughter. I am sure that when he woke up this morning he would have had no idea how his day would end. I started feeling sorry for him.

He came out casually and looked around for his car. He couldn't find it because Ganesh and his goons had pulled the car away from the college gate to a more deserted location, though still visible. And then, after a few minutes of looking around, Aman spotted it a few hundred yards away from where he had initially parked. Surprised, he started walking towards it. Poor guy knew nothing of what was coming for him. Secretly, I wished he would run away from Ganesh and Sidharth; no one deserved what he was about to go through.

Minutes later, he was in front of his car, four bikes and twelve people blocking his way.

'Uhh . . .' he said. 'What . . . is all this?'

'I will tell you bacchha, what is all this,' Ganesh said, as he walked towards him. 'Do you know him?' And he pointed to Sidharth. He patted Aman's face, more like slapped it.

'Sidharth? What . . . what are you doing . . . here? And look, I am . . . sorry . . . I . . .' he stuttered and stammered. Ganesh looked at him, smiled, and stepped back as Sidharth walked up to him, his eyes firmly stuck on him. Aman looked like he was staring right at his death, and he wasn't far from the truth either. Please don't kill him, I said to myself.

'Take this,' Ganesh said and handed over the iron knuckle to Sidharth.

Aman looked at the knuckle and his face looked like he was about to cry. He would get no mercy that day.

'Too late for an apology, buddy,' Sidharth said.

'But . . .'

That was the only sound that came out his mouth before Sidharth's iron-knuckled fist went smashing into his upper jaw and blood splattered on the ground. Once, twice, thrice. He stumbled on the ground. As he staggered to his feet, blood dripping from his mouth, Sidharth swung his heel on his shin, breaking his stance and sending him crashing to the ground again. He caught the man by his hair and spat on his face. Aman turned on his side and had just started to say something, bleeding from his nose and mouth, when Sidharth kicked him in the ribs twice with crushing force. Aman curled into a ball on the ground. Satisfied, Sidharth walked away, smiling at Ganesh.

'All yours,' he said to him, giving him the bloodstained iron knuckle back.

Seconds later, five men were kicking Aman right in the ribs where Sidharth had first hit him. After a while, with blood splattered across his face and his shirt and the ground on which he lay, he passed out.

Ganesh stripped him, threw his car keys and his clothes in the gutter nearby, punctured all his tyres, smashed the windows and the rear view mirrors and left him bleeding there. I just wished he wouldn't *die* there. He wouldn't. It wasn't Ganesh's first time. Though I hoped it would be the last for me.

I can never get these images out of my head; the first few punches that had landed on that guy's face and the spattering of blood all over the car wasn't as scary as the ferocious animal cries that Sidharth had let out while hitting him. We went back home and Sidharth washed his bloodied clothes and hands. He was *smiling*. A sense of calm pervaded his face.

'He won't die, right?' I asked.

He laughed.

That was the day I learnt to fear being on the wrong side of love. It's dangerous and it's damaging. You can find yourself naked in an empty street with a few missing teeth, and it's a high price to pay for love.

'What if there is a police case?' I asked him.

'You think I am that stupid?' Sidharth asked. 'Aman is a *nobody*. Ganesh rules the streets. *Nobody* can touch him. And as a result nobody can touch *me*.'

'But what if he comes with men of his own and comes after you,' I asked, a little fearful.

'I would really like him to try and do that. Because I think I would like to have another go at this guy. In fact, I would love it if he comes and tries that. Maybe next time around, you can swing in a few kicks, too,' he laughed. 'You told me you would stand next to me, but all you did was stand in the corner like a pussy.'

'Oh? Was I? Didn't you see me do my cheerleader dance while you were beating him to death? This wasn't funny, and it was fucking dangerous.'

'I said the same to myself when I got cheated on—*not funny*,' he said.

'But what did you get out of it?'

'Vani will always think of me whenever she sees his ugly face.'

I had nothing to say to that. We never heard from Aman or Vani ever again. You don't cross a madman twice. Period.

***

'You guys are savages,' I said, horrified at what Joy had just told me.

'What? Me? I didn't do anything!' Joy defended himself.

'But you could have stopped them.'

'What? Stop Ganesh? No one messes with him. You know, when he left the scene, he scratched his name on the hood of the car just to tell the local police that it was his doing. No one can touch him . . .'

'But Sidharth? You could have persuaded him, he was your friend.'

'If you had seen him, you wouldn't say this. Those intense eyes, man,' he said. 'I was helpless! I am sure, had I said anything, he would have swung his fist at me, too.'

'Aww! Poor you. And I would certainly hate stitches across your dimple,' I said and pulled his cheeks. Joy always looked pretty average to me. The only part that I liked about his looks was the deep gash on his face—his dimple; he's a cute boy, but not my type.

'What next?' I asked.

'The first year of my engineering ended with that. And the second year went without any incident either. But as soon as the third year began, things began to happen.'

'What things?' I asked.

'My first true and everlasting love.'

'First love? What was Sheeny then?'

68

'There is a difference! That was my first true love. This one was supposed to be everlasting! I was so sure about this girl I had everything planned. Like long term, like really long term, like thinking of baby names and shit, typical movie stuff. She was everything to me!'

'You look so adorable right now as you say it.'

'As in?' he said.

'You look like you are in love!' I said.

'Shut up,' he said, a little embarrassed.

'Who was she?'

'Manika,' Joy said. 'Smarter than anyone I had ever met, funnier than anyone, hotter than anyone, better-looking than Aphrodite herself. She was a goddess! She was my love!'

The First True and
Everlasting Love—Part 1

The incident with Sidharth taught me two lessons—*Do a background check if you plan a fuck-up.*

Second—*Don't worry. Sidharth and Ganesh will always be there. Go, fuck-up!*

After Vani became history, Sidharth went back to his old ways, only this time around he was being a bigger asshole than earlier. He got into multiple relationships at a time, and dumped girls by the hour. It had been a year since the break-up and Sidharth's fling business just kept on rising; my advice to let it go fell on deaf ears. He used to hit on the most random girls possible. Facebook, supermarkets, clubs, pubs . . . he tried everything.

But then, one day, he found something that was better than all these places.

Private rave parties.

These were underground parties, mostly in garages in farmhouses, very covert and darn expensive; rich kids only. Often people weren't allowed to park their cars within a two-mile radius and had to take autos to get to that place.

No flashy clothes. Every precaution was taken to avoid the common man's eye. One had to pay upwards of ten thousand a night and know many important people (or be white) just to get into those packed garages with junkies sprawled across everywhere and smoking their brains out.

From LSD, mushrooms, ecstasy, acid and cocaine, to the lower drugs like charas and ganja, everything flowed freely there. Cash worth tens of lakhs changed hands in a single night. Sidharth had been going to these parties on a regular basis now, and I held out for a couple of months before I finally gave in (as you know by now, I have always been scared).

'C'mon, man. Let's go. It will be fun. You will like it,' Sidharth insisted.

'I can't! I just don't have that kind of money on me now,' I said. 'And I don't even drink, or smoke! I don't even know how to do any of those things, and if you ask me, you should stop going to those places as well.'

'Shut up, Mom. Don't worry about the money, my father just hit a purple patch, and who else is he earning for? I am paying.'

'I am not convinced he's earning for his son and his friend to attend raves,' I smirk.

'I think you should eat my dick, but for now, let's go!'

'I have no interest in drugs, man. And neither should you. Let's just hang out someplace else.'

'It's not about the drugs, asshole. It's about the women! They are scantily dressed, knocked out of their senses and they are falling all over each other! You have no idea how these girls behave after an ecstasy pill enters their bloodstream. They are like nymphomaniacs on their dying day. It's going to be great. Trust me.'

'Fine. I will come,' I said. 'Although it's not because of what you said, but because I want you to shut up talking like a pervert.'

'Look who's talking man! You're the one who dumped your ex-girlfriend after sleeping with her, and you sent her to Bangalore, far away from you just to get rid of her,' he mocked.

'Let's not go there,' I grumbled. He nodded.

I wasn't really excited, but I wanted to see if Sidharth was lying; usually he never did. It took us three hours to get there, and we ran out of petrol twice and I begged him to turn around but he said we were too close to go back now; I had nothing to say, and I am glad I didn't.

It was pretty late when we reached, and we were frisked and asked scores of questions, which Sidharth answered with ease, before the monstrous guards let us in. The gigantic basement of the farmhouse lit up in red and green and blue, was already teeming with people; music reverberated within the walls. The experience was something I had *never* imagined. Sidharth had described the place a million times earlier, but seeing it with my own eyes was a different experience altogether. People lay around like corpses, danced like zombies; it was *terrifying* in the beginning, it seemed straight out of a *Resident Evil* movie, and I thought people would start biting each other any moment, and well, some of them were doing exactly that, glazed eyes and all. For somebody like me who wasn't even into drinking, it was a shock.

'Have this!' Sidharth shouted.

'*What* is this?' I shouted back in his ear.

'Just *drink*!' he said and forced the drink down my throat. It tasted funny, pungent. Sidharth disappeared, smiling at me, waving thumbs-up signs and winking. Within minutes, I knew something was wrong. Sidharth disappeared and soon, I found myself in a crowd of swaying young men and women, many of whom were shirtless and sweating. Nobody seemed to have any sense of control as they all fell over each other, laughing, cursing. Bodies walked towards and collapsed on the couches kept in the corners. Zombies, I couldn't think of any other word that correctly described them, and also me. Slowly, the lights became vibrant and intense. I could almost feel the lights and sounds . . . I was soon fucking *high*, stoned or whatever it was; it felt great. I was flying over things, landing over things. It was freaking strange. Noise and extreme silence invaded my mind alternatively. I felt powerful, invincible.

Though after a while, I don't know how much because time is meaningless when you're high, nausea followed and I threw up twice in the washroom. Had I discovered where Sidharth was, I would have knocked his teeth out (kind of impossible, but I sure would have tried). My head felt like it would burst and lie splattered in my palms. I started to look for Sidharth and couldn't find him. There were people kissing and making out and licking each other's faces everywhere; it wasn't hot, it was disgusting.

The debauchery of the night just kept stepping up in tempo. Random girls making out with random boys, changing boys, two guys with a girl, two girls on a guy. And when I say making out, it *means* making out. Not cute stuff, but nasty stuff. *Shocking!*

Slowly, the nausea went away and I could walk straight without bumping into people. Had someone narrated this to me, I would have probably never believed it, but this happened right in front of my eyes. These places were run by very powerful people and run very secretly. Many of these joints happened to earn more in a night than a regular club earned in a month.

'First night here?' someone shouted in my ear. More than the sound, I felt the breath in my ears, it was warm.

'Yes,' I shouted back.

'No drugs?' she asked.

I shook my head. I looked at her and could only see her eyes and teeth glinting in the UV lights that lit up the place; she looked freaky.

'Good,' she shouted. 'Want to go out for some fresh air?'

She pointed at the gate and we started to walk towards it. Normally, I wouldn't go alone with any unknown girl (because I am a wimp), but that night called for heroics. Girls and guys were jumping all around us, trying to pull us into the crowd. We fought, pushed and made our way outside. The bouncers at the gate shook their heads and only let us out when she flashed a thousand rupee note. He let her go. As I tried to slip past the guard, he stopped me. *What?* A thousand bucks just to go out? I fished out the money from my wallet and gave it away reluctantly. *That's my three weeks' pocket money, you big, muscular asshole!*

'Why are you here?' she asked as she lit up her cigarette.

'A friend tagged me along. He has contacts and all.'

'Obviously he has,' she said and offered me a smoke. Immediately, I was intimidated by her presence. There is something about girls and smoking that always turns me on, maybe it's the fact that they are dying slowly and they are reckless at the same time; it's an interesting mix of sympathy and awe.

'Why are you here?' I asked, although going by her confidence, she looked like a regular at a place like this.

'The second girl you kissed today . . . that was my sister,' she said, without a change in expression.

'What? *I?* I didn't . . .'

'Yes, after that friend bought you that drink, you went around like a madman, grabbing and groping everybody. Don't be sorry about it, you obviously don't remember and I hold no grudges,' she said and took a puff, still very dispassionate about the whole incident. 'People are their real selves after they are high. Maybe you're just a deprived pervert.'

'I am NOT a deprived pervert! I am NOT,' I said, my voice trailed as I tried to remember what had happened.

'Stop thinking about it, it will not come back,' she said. 'It never does. It's called a blackout.'

What the fuck? She was reading my mind!

'So you are here with her?' I asked.

'She will go into rehab tomorrow. She wanted one last night here. I had to come with her,' she said. 'I would have never come to this place, bunch of stupid rich kids destroying their lives.'

'I am neither rich, nor am I destroying myself. And I am sorry I kissed your sister!' I defended myself.

'It's okay. She is as much to blame, and you were high so you didn't know any better. She's an addict,' she said and took a long drag, an uneasy silence descended.

'What do you do?'

'Apart from accompany my sister to raves and see her getting kissed by raging perverts, I am a journalist,' she said.

Right! *Journalist.* That is *not* what she looked like. Though she was dressed in a simple T-shirt and jeans like everyone that night, the kohl was still there, as if she was trying to support the cliché of *'journalist with kohl in her eyes'.* Her hair hung open loosely over her shoulders, thick as the night itself. She was very alluring and pleasing to look at beyond all the cigarette smoke. Her lips had a natural pout and she wore a very faint shade of pink lipstick; she was skinny, and yet not so. She looked more like a newsreader, the kind the channels choose to keep the TRPs up, knowing that millions would lose themselves every night watching her talk. Her eyes were immensely seductive, a little dreamy, but still very big and attention catching, a light shade of brown accentuated by the kohl in her eyes; I wondered if I was still high. Her left ear was pierced at three places and she wore three rings on each hand.

Standing in front of her, I could feel the motions of going from being intrigued to having a crush to falling in love, in a matter of a few brief minutes.

'So, your sister is an addict, eh?'

'It's been almost a year since she dropped out of college. She was in St. Stephen's. She was really good at academics. She took the same course as I did.'

St. Stephen's. Fuck. Be less impressive, girl!

'It didn't take us long to find out what was happening to her. We managed to convince her, and that's the only good part about it,' she mumbled, lighting up the cigarette dangling from her lips, her second.

It was amazing how her expression had not changed in the whole conversation, whereas I had gone from being amazed to being sad to being surprised to being shocked. And dumb at times, when I was checking her out. And that was almost *all* the time.

'This is where it all started?' I asked, out of sheer curiosity.

'This is where she first tried it.'

'. . . and kept coming back?'

'*No*, you have to be a certified junkie to get in here. No one here wants a rookie who will just come once, click pictures and put them on the Internet. These places are for the *needy*. For people who come here for the drugs. The music, the sex and everything else is just secondary,' she explained.

'It must be a great story for a journalist, such clubs. I would have never believed they exist, had I not seen this one today.'

'Yes, it's a great story that must never be published, unless of course, someone wants to be found dead under *mysterious* circumstances. Everyone powerful is in on it. Three people tried it and all of them lost their jobs and the stories never got printed. And anyway, I not an investigative journalist, I write about books and food and art. Sometimes, when I really get bored, I also cover page three,' she sounded mysterious, sexy, friendly, authoritative . . . everything good, all at the same time.

'Scary,' I said and realized I just can't stop being a scared-ass wimp. 'I mean not the other part, the first part, about the raves.'

'Seeing your sister make out with a black bouncer is scary. Seeing her cry out in the middle of the night for drugs is scarier,' she said. This time, I saw tears in her eyes. 'Anyway, what do you do?'

'I'm still studying, second year, Engineering.'

'Ohh, you're a kid,' she said condescendingly.

'Not really. I dropped a year in between. You don't look all that old yourself,' I was a little offended by the comment.

'I am twenty-two,' she said.

'You sound thirty,' I said.

'Not funny.'

'Neither were you.'

'Aha! The kid has *teeth*,' she said and laughed. 'I like that in a boy.'

'I will look out for your articles in the newspapers and see how grown-up you are!' I said.

'You wouldn't understand. I review literary books. You wouldn't get anything. You should stick with your calculus books,' she smirked.

'What! I read books. I mean, a few,' I said. 'Oh, don't pull that I-am-from-St-Stephens-so-I-am-so-much-smarter-than-you thing on me!'

She laughed and said, 'But I am.'

We talked for a few more minutes, after which the skies started getting clearer and we headed back to the dark garage, much to my disappointment. It was pretty much the same, only that a lot more people had passed out and were sleeping heaped over one another in corners. She looked around for her sister, while I looked around for Sidharth amongst the bodies.

'There,' she shouted and pointed to a corner, where Sidharth lay with his mouth open over a white-skinned girl who was still bobbing her head to the music. As I walked towards him, the *mysterious* journalist girl walked up to an equally good-looking girl . . . Wait, they almost looked alike! They had a short argument and a few moments later, she dragged her sister out of the place. She passed me a fleeting smile as she passed by.

Fuck! And then, it struck me, I didn't ask her name, or where she worked or anything about it. Though, the full realization struck much later. I had dragged Sidharth out of that club, into an auto, then into the car and then onto his bed. I must have slapped him, punched him, threatened to leave him on the road a zillion times to make him wake up, but *nothing* worked.

Had it not been for that rude girl from St. Stephen's, it would've been a horrible night. And an even more horrible morning, carrying a huge unconscious man around. I was lucky Sidharth's mom didn't catch me carrying her son upstairs to his room.

As he lay unconscious, I tried sleeping, but couldn't fall asleep. Probably attributed to her face that I just couldn't get out of my head. I switched on the laptop and mindlessly searched for porn on Sidharth's laptop to kill time. Her words echoed in my ears, 'You're a deprived pervert!' No I am not, I said to myself, and clicked on the play button. The girl in the porn had just started unbuckling the belt of the buffed up guy, when slowly her face transformed into *her* face—the journalist girl! *Darn! Fuck.* I clicked on another. And the same thing happened again. *Am I still high?*

I wasn't. I went on to the Internet as I thought about her and relived the conversation. To feel better, I even added to it, imagining that I had asked for her name or her phone number. I lay back daydreaming about her. That dense wavy flowing hair, those eyes that seemed even bigger with the kohl around them, the smoky-fair complexion was as exotic as it was pleasing. I imagined her in her journalist attire and she looked *awesome*.

Within moments, I was onto the page three columns and book review columns of about a dozen newspapers. I noted down all the names of the female correspondents that I could and started searching them on Facebook. An hour and half later, and after checking out hundreds of profiles, I came up blank. *Nothing.* Tired and with hurting eyes, I lay down on the bed, thinking about her, and drifted off. She was there, in my dreams, laughing at me for being a crude engineer-to-be, and was throwing her big, literary books at me.

* * *

'You couldn't find her?' I said, almost a little frustrated. 'And why the fuck didn't you ask her name?'

'I don't know,' Joy answered, a little foxed himself. 'I was just too lost, I guess. She was excessively beautiful, Neeti. And frankly, it didn't cross my mind. I really didn't think it would get so hard to get her out of my head.'

'And why didn't you tell her that you read a lot of books too! I mean you're always surrounded by books, you're obsessed with them. You had something common there, didn't you?'

'I guess I was a little intimidated. And even though I read a lot, I am not sure I understand them totally,' he said. As usual, he was pulling himself down and being self-deprecating.

'Then how did you meet her again? Did you go back there again? Ohh . . . wait . . . you visited rehabilitation centres to see who checked in and that's how you got it? Oh . . . wait, wait, wait, the bouncer, he knew her? Didn't he?' I kept guessing.

'Wrong. Wrong. And wrong.'

'Then what?' I asked, impatiently.

'It was a lot less dramatic,' he said. 'I guess I was just insanely lucky again. Or maybe it was fate.'

* * *

The First True and Everlasting Love—Part 2

'*Wake up*! Wake up, asshole.' My ears rung for five minutes before I opened my eyes and saw Sidharth shouting at me.

'Are you fucking out of your mind?' I shouted and turned around. I would have punched him but I didn't want to get punched in return.

I must have slept for another hour or so, after which I woke up to the aroma of smoking hot pizzas that Sidharth had ordered. Almost immediately, I forgave him and dug in, stuffing whole slices inside my mouth. The pizza disappeared in seconds, almost as if they never existed.

'I am sorry for last night,' he said, not even meaning it.

'Glad you realized.'

'But it was a one-time go, you have to admit that! C'mon, you had fun, and I didn't know you would grind and do all those dirty moves. You're such a pervert!' Sidharth smirked.

'Fuck you,' I said and flipped the newspaper. *Am I a pervert?*

'But you did like it?' he winked.

'I met someone,' I said.

'I saw! You met *many* someones! You kissed at least three girls yesterday, Joy.'

'Can we stop talking about what I did after I was drunk? And you weren't the perfect model of sincerity either! Anyway, I meant I talked to someone yesterday after I came to my senses.'

'Who?'

'I don't know her name. But I intend to find out soon. She's a journalist and writes about books and art and page three parties.'

'You don't know her? You didn't ask her name? Anyway, Joy, you better stay away from these junkie girls. They are real twisted. Don't get into all this. Soon, you will be paying for their drugs!'

'She wasn't a junkie. She came there with her sister,' I said, casually flipping through the paper.

'What's so special about her?'

'I don't know,' I said, not knowing what to say. And then, suddenly—when I wasn't even looking for it, or even if anyone was, I don't think they would have found it—in a hazy picture on page three, somewhere in the background, I saw a familiar face. *There she was! There she fucking was! Oh my fucking god! Unreal!*

Barely visible, but I was sure it was *her*. Sure as hell, it was her. I noted the email-id in my head, rechecked and rechecked . . . it was she. All this time, Sidharth looked at me, clueless as to what I was doing.

'What the fuck?' Sidharth shouted, as I rushed to get his laptop.

I read it a zillion times before sending it.

Hi

It's me. The new guy in the club. How did I find you? Pure chance, if you would believe it. How's the sister?

Joy Datta

P.S.—0967999996

'You met her yesterday? And you are *mailing* her? Have you gone totally nuts? Mailing a junkie? And you do know that the mail was a little desperate!' he said, his eyes glued to the newspaper, trying to see what I saw.

'Firstly, she is *not* a junkie, her sister is. I think she was very pretty. I liked her. And was the mail too desperate? Was it?'

'Maybe. You *so* sound like you are going to fall in love,' he said. 'You do know what love does to guys like us, right? It ends in tears and it feels like the world is ending!'

'Shut up, dude.'

'And moreover I think she is too good for you,' Sidharth said, as he munched on a biscuit. 'She is a journalist and writes high-brow stuff, and you're, like, nothing. You're not even good-looking!'

'Says the guy who is ten kilograms overweight. And how can you say she's out of my league? You haven't even met her.'

'You tell me that she is good-looking. Now, you have always been with women you don't deserve. *Sarah*—out of your league. *Sheeny*—out of your league. So looks-wise—she is out of your league. And she is a journalist, older and wiser, and earning. And she had the balls to be there, at that party . . . that means she definitely has more balls than you have,' he said, as he gulped his coffee down.

'You are ridiculous. I mean, she is . . . well, out of my league, but it's not that she is un-gettable. I mean, *why* are we talking about it? I just want to meet her once. I found her nice. And that's it. End of story,' I said and he laughed aloud.

'Whatever, man,' Sidharth said. 'I hope you get her. Which obviously you won't.'

I spent the rest of the day at his place checking my mail inbox as frequently as anyone could. It was all I could do. Mom called up and asked when I would come home, and I gave her some lame excuse and she disconnected the call. Sidharth was obviously not impressed with my freaky behaviour. It was early evening when it bore fruit.

The subject line said—*Hi*.

The body of the mail said—*0798989889*.

If anything, the mail was a little disturbing. *Nothing else?* Just a number. Almost involuntarily, I looked around for my cell phone. Not calling would have looked cooler, I guess, but as soon as I saw the number, I didn't give a shit. I just had to call her. It was a reflex!

'Hey,' I said, my voice almost shaking initially.

'Who's this?' her voice boomed from the other side.

'Joy.'

'Hey, hi! How are you? By the way, I LOVE your name. It's so Bengali, and it's too intelligent for you,' she chuckled.

'*Haha!* Very funny. How are you?' I said, and left it there.

'I am good. I just dropped my sister at the rehab facility. Driving back. The jam near Safdarjung is killing, man. I think I will just park and let it all clear out.'

'Safdarjung? I am in Safdarjung right now, at a friend's place . . . umm . . . err . . . Can we—?'

'Great then. See you at Barista, SDA market, in five minutes? That's fine by you?'

How can it not be fine with me?

'Fine, I will be there,' I said and cut the phone.

Sidharth, who had overheard the entire conversation, said,'Lucky bastard. *Fuck* you man. You got yourself a date? I hope you're run over by a truck. Or wait, I hope you fall in love, that's much worse.'

'Fuck you.'

'Fuck you more, fuck you twice, and then fuck you again. I hope you die, man,' he said.

'I will try not to disappoint you.'

'Whatever. Try not falling in love for a change! It never works out for us,' he joked.

Yes. I did fall in love *very* often, but in my defence, I fell out of it with alarming frequency, too, often finding myself descending into a downward spiral of depression. Anyway, luckily I found something decent from Sidharth's wardrobe to wear and made a mad dash to the market. SDA market was bang opposite IIT, Delhi, and despite that, the crowd was always decent; the market had a smattering of a few very nice restaurants (expensive!) and though I didn't go there often, I had heard a lot about it.

I found her sitting at the corner table, engrossed in a newspaper. She still looked resplendent, even better than the night before. The aura of intrigue and mysteriousness still hung in the air around her, like a shroud. I took a deep breath, put on my most confident smile and walked up to her. *You look okay*, I lied to myself.

'Hey. Sad traffic, eh?' I said.

'You bet,' she said. 'But then, we wouldn't have met.'

'True, that,' I said and pulled myself a chair.

'By the way, I took the liberty of ordering you a cappuccino. I hope you don't mind. They were about to kick me out. I had to order something. It's strange that they wouldn't let a girl sit in their coffee shop, that's behaviour they reserve for boys.'

'Cappuccino is fine,' I said.

'But you're paying, right?' she chuckled. 'Oh wait, you're still a student! I wouldn't want you to spend your pocket money.'

'Okay, *Mom*! Why don't you buy me stuff or I will hold my breath?'

'That's a nice comeback, Joy. That's unexpected.'

'Thank you! I have been practising,' I said and smiled. *So far, so good.*

'So, how did you find me?' she asked. 'I mean, it's a little strange to be contacted by a guy who knows nothing about you, exactly one day after you meet him at a rave.'

'It wasn't that tough. Got up this morning, saw the newspaper, spotted a shadow of yours in the background, and mailed you.'

'Aha? That simple, haan?' she said.

I smiled. The way she said it made me feel like she knew that I was lying and there was more to it.

'Okay, *not* really. I kicked myself all morning for not asking your name. But then, I remembered that you said you cover page three events and book reviews. So, I tracked down every page three journalist and tried to find them on Facebook. Nothing fit. But then, I saw today's newspaper and saw you in the background!' I said.

'That's flattering. And cute,' she said and chuckled. 'And you do know that you are desperate, right?'

'Yes, a lot of people say that. But a guy as ugly as me has to take his chances,' I said.

'C'mon. Joy. You are *not* ugly. What makes you say so?'

'The mirror,' I said. 'I have five mirrors at my place, and all concur.'

'Bullshit,' she said. 'I love your name by the way, *Joy,*' she said. 'Joy. Joy. Joy,' she repeated it a few times. 'It has a nice ring to it.'

'Thank you,' I smiled sheepishly. 'So how long does your sister stay in rehab?'

'About six months to start with. Let's see. It was pretty hard today. If there is one thing in the world that I choose above myself, it is her. And I wonder how I didn't see it coming . . . She was right there in front of me, going to parties, I just . . . and . . . never . . . thought . . .' her voice cracked.

'I hope everything gets straightened out,' I said.

'*Everyone* says that. I just hope it just does,' she sipped her coffee. 'How is that friend of yours doing?'

'He is good. That's where I was. He lives nearby.'

'Ohh, that's cool,' she said. 'Does he know you're meeting me here?'

'Yes. He asked me to be careful and he hopes that I die.'

'Careful? *Why?*'

'He says I will fall in love.'

'Aha! Will you?'

'If you keep being this charming, I might,' I said and she smiled.

We talked for another hour and she told me about her unending collection of books, her love for hardbound novels, and then we discussed books and her favourite authors, and her job and her colleagues, her sister and how much she loved her, and she asked me about college and Sidharth and whether I was dating somebody. I told her about Sarah and Sheeny, and she told me that I was a little, lost kid, and I couldn't help but agree. And then she received a call from her office and had to go. She hugged me when she left and thanked me for being there. When I asked her why, she said it was because she was in a rotten mood and I had helped her see through it. I had no idea how.

'See you soon then?' she said, as she was leaving.

'Sure,' I said. 'How soon?' I asked and I wished sound waves were not waves, but particles and I hoped I could stop them from reaching her.

'Excuse me?' she said and smiled.

'Nothing, nothing.'

'I heard that,' she said. 'After office today? Seven o' clock?'

'Seven. Okay.'

'You are free?' she asked. 'Oh, I forgot, you're a student. I hope I don't eat into your playtime.'

'Whatever.'

She smiled and said she would text me the place. She walked away and drove off. I smiled to myself. This was going better than I had ever imagined.

~

'You bastard!' Sidharth exclaimed. 'You are going out with her again? She asked you out or you did?'

'I don't know. I guess we both did,' I said.

'I don't believe you. You couldn't have asked her out, you would have rather pissed your pants. So how's she? Better than last night? Girls usually look better after sundown.'

'She was so much better. She's so pretty and smart. We even like the same books!'

'Oh. My. God. Shut up and stop thinking about having

kids with her already. You're like a little school girl, man,' Sidharth mocked. 'So, did you click a picture?'

'What? No, I didn't!' I said.

Sidharth mocked me and compared me to women who scream for boy bands, sparkly vampires and the like, after a while, his enthusiasm died and he got back to his porn and his PlayStation. I, on the other hand, had a tough time counting hours and checking my phone for her text and at around six, she texted me to ask if I could reach Connaught Place in half an hour. Apparently, she had got free from her office earlier than usual. Though she said it was okay if I made it by seven, but what she didn't know was that I would die—DIE—to spend an extra half hour with her.

'Would you drive me to CP?' I asked Sidharth.

'*What?*' he asked and put his game on pause. He wasn't doing so well, his team, Arsenal, was getting beaten by a lesser known team. 'I am not going anywhere.'

'C'mon, man! It's urgent, she's waiting. I came with you to your stupid party; you got to do this for me.'

'You are going on this date because of the stupid party, asshole!' he argued.

'You know what I mean, Sidharth.'

After a few minutes of persuasion, he said yes, but only if I introduced him to her, too. He wanted to see the girl who had been driving me nuts since the last eighteen hours. Eighteen hours? It seemed a lot longer, more on the lines of eternity. We hopped onto the bike and reached CP in twenty minutes and waited where she had asked us to. Sidharth told me he would kick my ass if the girl fell short of what I had described her as, smart and gorgeous.

'Hey!' a voice screamed out. I looked behind and there she was, sitting on the pavement, smoking her cigarette. 'Come. Sit,' she said.

'Is that her?' Sidharth whispered in my ear and I nodded. 'She is amazing! Die in hell, Joy, IN HELL,' he said and squeezed my arm. *I know.*

'Are you guys talking about me?' she asked and thrust out her hand. 'Hi. Manika.'

'Sidharth,' he said.

'So, what was he saying?' Manika asked me.

'He just said that you were amazing and he wished I would die in hell,' I said.

'Well, thank you,' she said and smiled at Sidharth.

'Pleasure,' he said. 'Anyway, you two have fun. I have some work, so I will go and do that.'

'Ohh, you have to go, right? I am sure it's very important,' Manika said and winked. 'This is so high-school type, you leaving the two of us alone. But then, you guys are about that age, aren't you?'

'Your girlfriend is very smart, Joy. I don't like it,' Sidharth smiled.

'I wish she were my girlfriend, and she will not be if you don't get lost,' I grumbled, and we laughed. He got on his bike, bid us goodbye and drove away, his bike thundering. And almost immediately, my phone beeped.

'I can bet my kidney on it that it's Sidharth,' she said, puffing on her cigarette.

'What if it's not?' I said.

'Anything you want,' she said. 'What if it is? Okay, if it is you will have to show me the message.'

'Deal.'

She laughed out pretty loud after reading the message:

If you don't get this girl, I will personally cut off your balls and draw fake boobs on you. And she is, as I said, out of your league. Get her. And tell her that I like her sister. I am sure if Manika is this hot, her sister would be too!

'Funny guy,' I said. 'Thank god for my kidney.'

'What had you told him about me?' she said.

'Nothing much, just that you're pretty, smart and funny, the usual, and that you're a journalist and you love books and art.'

'I am glad you didn't miss out anything,' she said and stubbed out her cigarette.

'You always wanted to be a journalist?' I asked her.

'Well, not really. It appealed to me then, but not anymore. I liked writing and I could never write a novel myself, and journalism was the next best thing.'

'Why don't you write a book? You're an avid reader, and you already write so you have the two required prerequisites to be a writer!' I said.

'Maybe. *Someday.* I don't think anyone would read it. And I am not able enough to write a literary book. I don't want to write for adults, you know, I like reading them but I think a lot of it is really pretentious and make-belief. I want to write a young-adult book, something that people my age can connect to,' she said and smiled. 'I think I am boring you. You always wanted to be an engineer?'

'Not really, but I never WANTED to be anything. Engineering is what all middle-class guys do. Engineering, Management. *Naukri.*'

'*Aww!* But there must be something, right? If you were to do something for the rest of your life and be paid for it, what would it be?'

'Never thought about it,' I said. 'I have always been too busy with entrance examinations and coaching classes. I think a well-paying, comfortable job, that's all I want.'

'Hmmm,' she said. She wasn't impressed.

I told her that I thought one has to be rich to have big dreams, and she was disappointed that I thought so. Manika was slightly well off, her dad worked in a big oil company and raked in quite some money. But she had never been the spendthrift type. Despite a new gleaming car, she always preferred the metro more; she *hated* the traffic.

I couldn't stop asking questions, and she entertained all of them with a patient smile on her lips. She told me she loved Chinese food and puppies and coffee and YouTube, and whistling during movies, that she has never missed watching any Shah Rukh Khan or Ben Affleck movie, that she hates her ex-boyfriends, and given a choice she would strangulate her boss; I started to love the things she loved too. I liked that she loved reading books and that she wanted to write one, that she blamed herself for what happened to her sister, and that she thought there was something I would want to do in life beyond having a comfortable job.

'Should we go somewhere else? It's a little cold here?' she said, as she got up from the pavement. It had been two hours since we had started talking. Her cheeks had turned red from the cold, and she pulled a muffler over her neck. She looked so painfully gorgeous in those moments that I wished that time would freeze for a little while, so that I could just look at her. As we walked away from that pavement, she held my arm to shield herself from the cold wind and I instinctively put my arm around her. She looked at me with those big brown eyes and Sidharth's words rang true in my head, 'You are falling in love again, Joy.'

It was the *greatest* feeling in the world. It filled my heart with joy that just can't be put into words. I wished to bump into every friend of mine, just so that everyone could see whom I was with right now. The. Prettiest. Girl. Ever.

* * *

'That easy, huh?' I said.

'Fate,' Joy said.

'So? What next? You asked her out? Or another date? Or did something happen on that date?' I asked, my curiosity peaking.

'Nothing happened. Other than the fact that she broke my heart into countless pieces.'

'What?'

'Yep. That's what happened. Just when I was looking at her sitting in that Japanese restaurant chewing on disgusting sushi that she ordered, imagining my entire life with her, she just went ahead and broke my heart into tiny little unsalvageable fragments. But then again, I don't blame her; she had not asked me to be smitten. I was just being stupid,' he said wistfully.

'Will you just shut up and tell me what happened?'

'She had a boyfriend,' he said.

'What? She had a boyfriend? Why didn't she tell you that before?' I asked, a little surprised

'Because I had not asked her.'

'But she should have told you!'

'That's what Sidharth said, too. I vowed not to call her again after that ridiculously wonderful date.'

'Then what?'

94

'Nothing much. Just depression . . . Just plain depression. I cried and cried and cried,' he said.

'You're such a cry-baby, Joy,' I remarked.

'I have been told,' he answered and continued.

The First True and Everlasting Love—Part 3

'No, you can't be serious. You are serious? *Wait?* Are you serious?' Sidharth said, visibly shocked when I broke the news to him. Quite obviously, his reaction was a lot less extreme than mine was. I was fuming, sad, depressed, angry and suicidal all at the same time. And yes, I cried.

I took a deep breath and said, 'I am serious. It's not her fault. It's not as if she was hiding it or anything. She just didn't feel it was *necessary* to tell me. And if it makes things any better, she even asked me if I had a girlfriend.'

'Just so you know,' Sidharth said, 'it doesn't make this okay. So what are you going to do about it?'

'Nothing.'

'Nothing? Joy! *True love!* This is what you don't find every day. I mean normal people don't find it every day. You are different. You find it every day,' he digressed.

'Stop it.'

'Okay, but seriously, this girl was different. You should go out and get her. And did I tell you that Ganesh called? We can take her boyfriend out from the equation, too.

Nobody would know. What do you say?' he said, all pumped up and excited.

'We are doing nothing of that sort,' I said and dug my head into my pillow. I cried.

'You are not even going to call her?'

'I don't think so,' I said.

'You disappoint me,' he said. 'You're such a girl!'

'*Fuck off*. If Mom calls, tell her I am sleeping here. Project work.'

'Whatever.'

I didn't call her.

~

A few weeks passed by and I was back to the drudgery of my normal life without that beautiful face tormenting me day-after-night-after-day. Yes, she called. She even called and asked me if we could meet up sometime. Though my heart just begged my mind to let go and meet her, I always came up with some pretext not to. It was a good decision not to meet her. I knew I would have fallen more in love with her every time I saw her. *How could I have not?* So, I tried my best to stay away from her. She was trouble.

Yes, sometimes I did check the newspaper and some social networking sites for traces of her and found many, but I exercised total self-restraint. I read her book reviews and would imagine her curled up on a couch with a book in her lap and a cup of coffee in her hands, spectacles perched precariously on her head, and I wondered if she ever thought of me.

I even started dating again—just an odd date here and there, nothing serious—and tried hard to get over her, but I was looking for her in every girl I met. It was a very *different* feeling, though. I wasn't really sad that I wasn't with her, though I knew that I would be the happiest guy if it were otherwise.

Oddly, I still felt thankful for that night and the day after, because for however short a period it was, the time I had spent with her was the best eighteen hours of my life. And it wasn't my fault either that she had a boyfriend. So it was all fine. I missed her face, her smile, the sound of her laughter, but whenever it came back to me, I couldn't help but smile and feel lucky that it had happened. A few months passed, and I stopped checking her Facebook profile. It wasn't as if I wasn't still in love with her, I just accepted it as a relationship that didn't work out and I got dumped. Sometimes I just looked into the mirror and smiled at my superpower to be so stupidly in love. I knew from that moment that life would never be the same. It was gut-wrenching, but I knew she would always be there, *those eighteen hours would always be there.*

~

'So, where do we go tonight?' Sidharth asked.

His father was on another one of his moneymaking streaks. The Sensex was doing well, and so was his father. It meant a lot of free luxuries for me. I didn't mind and I prayed for his father to be the next Harshad Mehta without the scam, or without any Ponzi scheme.

'TGIF?' I said.

'Sure. Whatever you say, man,' he said and we drove on.

We ordered nachos and pastas and well-done chicken and he ate with a vengeance. He was working out hard these days and it was the only day in the week that he really ate like a guy as big as him should.

'Joy,' he said. 'Do you remember the last time we went to college?'

'We did. Last week? *Why?*' I asked.

'Do you *hear* what you are saying?'

'What?'

'We don't attend classes! I don't think we have ever attended more than a lecture a day!' he said. 'That's sad, that's not how it should be.'

'What's your point?'

'We are *fucking* up our careers. People slog day-after-night-after-day and all we do is this . . . eat and talk about girls, go back home and sleep. That's not the life we want to lead, man.'

'But we pass all our exams and our scores are above sixty per cent, and that's makes us pretty awesome, I think,' I said.

Life at Delhi College of Engineering had been a cakewalk. The attendance was never really a worry and now that we were in the latter half of our engineering days, things had become even simpler. The exams were considerably easy, the professors left us alone, and we were seniors, so we had settled comfortably in our roles in the social pecking order and weren't as unsure as we were as juniors when we constantly battled the fears of being uncool (and often lost!).

'I was thinking something else,' he said. 'You know, there is a provision that you can do the last three semesters in a foreign university if you get accepted. And it's on full scholarship. Everything is paid for, be it lodging, tuition fee, and even flight tickets! Imagine that.'

'Yeah, but all the seniors that went last year were like little geniuses! They had projects and recommendations and the professors loved them. It's not like we have a chance.'

'We *can*. I still have one semester to go. The applications are to be submitted at the end of the semester. So I still have a few months left to work on my profile. I was thinking of taking up some projects under a few professors and giving it a shot. I will apply for some improvement examinations and get my percentage up by a few points. What do you say?' he asked.

It was strange to hear such talk from him. Two years of engineering had passed by and he had not said a word about studies and suddenly he wanted to do extra projects, give re-examinations and apply to foreign universities. It was awkward.

'If you want to do it, then why not?' I said.

'Why don't you try for it too?'

'*Naah*, I will try to go for management exams a year after I pass out from here. So, the whole foreign university thing doesn't fit into my profile. If you haven't noticed, I never wanted to do engineering,' I said, a little worried now. Sidharth was suddenly getting serious about his life and career. I wished him luck, though I really didn't like this new Sidharth. He was scary and he was making me feel worthless. Being happy for him was one thing, but scaring the shit out of me by getting serious about life was another thing altogether. I *had* to do something, too. I thought of Manika and the time she said, 'There must be something that you want to do?'

Unfortunately, I was a lost kid.

~

During the next week, Sidharth went up to a few professors to ask if they were heading projects he could be a part of and contribute. They had *never* seen him, and the few who had weren't kind to him. I used to stand outside their offices, hearing all the nasty things that they said to him but he didn't back out and kept begging for projects; he told them he was ready to even wash beakers or scour for sponsorships. After trying his luck with twenty-odd professors, he finally found one who didn't exactly give him a project but gave him the permission to help a senior of ours with a project that he was working on. I hadn't really seen Sidharth taking so much shit from anyone, let alone old professors, so all of this was very uncanny.

'Hey,' Sidharth said, as he came out from the professor's room. 'I got a project.'

'Yeah. I heard that,' I said. 'I can't say I am very happy for you. Why exactly are you doing this? These are the same fucking professors you have grown up cursing, dude.'

'I told you. Three-semester vacation at a foreign university! What else?'

'You can't get me with that. Tell me. What's bothering you? And don't tell me it suddenly struck you that you're wasting your life!' I asked.

He thought about it for a little while and said, 'I had a fight with Dad a few days back.'

'And?'

'Remember a year ago we had thrashed that guy? Aman. Vani's ex-boyfriend?' he said.

'Yes, how can I forget? One year, eh? Seems like yesterday,' I said.

'It turns out his father works for the same firm as my father's. He was home a few days back . . . with Aman.'

'You are kidding,' I said. '*How* did he know that you are . . . you know that your father . . .? Whatever. How did he know of the connection?'

'He didn't. They had just casually dropped in. Aman was shocked to see me. And so was I. He said nothing then, but the next day at office, my dad was on the receiving end of some nasty comments.'

'What?'

'Aman's father told Dad all about what had happened. He called Dad names too. And the next morning, Dad gave it to me in equal measure. Dad said he had never been proud of me. He said I was worthless and wished I was never born. You know how parents are,' he said, head hung low, walking listlessly.

'And you think this whole project thing will fix that?' I asked.

'I don't know, but at least I can try to make it better. Give him at least one reason to feel proud because apparently I have failed them as a son. Also, a lot of Dad's friend's sons are doing great in their lives, they are going to IITs and Harvard and Boston while I just drive around Delhi on my stupid bike with you.'

'Excuse me?' I punched him.

'You know what I mean,' he responded.

'You're one unlucky asshole. Pretty small world, eh?'

'Yes. It sure is,' he said.

No wonder his mood had been off for the last few days. His parents had said some pretty ugly things—and parents always dig out old mistakes and follies long forgotten—and he wanted to prove himself now. Sidharth had *never* taken shit from anyone, and the only reason he was taking so much from the oldies at the college was because he didn't want any of it from his own parents!

'But you do know that I am going to get bored if you spend so much time on projects,' I said ruefully. I knew anyone who took up such projects ended up working their asses off; their social lives became non-existent, revolving around numbers, calculations and engines.

'C'mon, man. I will take time out for you.'

'It is better that you don't. I want you to see this one through,' I said. 'In fact, let me join my CAT coaching too. Then we can at least study together. That should be fun. What say?'

'Are you serious?' he asked me.

'I have to join those classes anyway. I will join it now,' I said. 'I'm not sure how studying together can be fun, but yeah, we can give it shot.'

'Cool. Then let's go now,' he said.

'*Now?* Where?'

'What? Where? To get you enrolled. I heard they are doing a special DCE discount this week. It's massive. Ten thousand off just for students from DCE,' he said, as he revved up the bike.

'And how do you know that?'

'I keep my eyes and ears open, man,' he said.

'I am not too kicked about the DCE batch. Why would I want the same people that I study with in college in a coaching class with me?' I asked, the idea of studying already felt repulsive.

'*Let's be nerds again!*'

As soon as he said that, the old Joy flashed in my head, fat, ugly and revolting, and I wondered if he had changed at all.

~

'Ma'am,' Sidharth said. 'Ma'am,' he repeated. 'Ma'am,' he said for the third time, trying to catch the attention of the kind lady at the reception who was juggling two phones, new admission forms and the timetables of old students all at the same time.

'Hi,' she said.

'Ma'am! We've been standing here for the last fifteen minutes!' he said rudely.

'What are you here for?' she asked.

'New admission,' he said.

'I will just get back to you in a while. Why don't you sit there and fill up the form like everyone else,' she pointed out to the waiting couches where quite a few people were doing the same.

'They will lose business if they keep treating potential students like this,' Sidharth said loud enough so that she could hear it.

'Let's just fill it up,' I said and pushed him away from the counter. We sat in a corner, huddled up with the other applicants, and started filling the form up. Sidharth picked out a management magazine and started reading; soon he started pointing out management jargon and laughed at the stupidity of it all.

'Will you just shut up?' I told him.

'It's funny, man! These kids spend tons of dollars studying finance and then blow the economy. How dumb is that!'

'You guys make aircrafts that crash and kill people, so shut your mouth and let me fill this up, Sidharth,' I retorted.

Just as I finished filling up the education column, I heard someone call out my name. I looked at the receptionist and it was not her. She was still juggling phones and students. 'Joy?' she said. 'Oh, my God! It's you. Hi! How are you?' she smiled.

Fuck! It was the face again. Manika Taneja.

'Hey, Manika,' I said. 'I am good. Good. Very good! How are you?'

Sidharth looked up and waved at her.

'Hi, Sidharth!' she said, smiling. Ah, that enchanting smile again!

'So, what are you guys doing here?'

'Oh, nothing, we are just thinking of buying this place out. So just filling up a form for that,' Sidharth had come to kind of hate her after the whole *I-have-a-boyfriend* incident. 'Why are you here, Manika? Outbid us? A word of caution, we have lots of money!'

'Shut up, Sidharth. I am enrolling myself. Third year engineering, so it's kind of time to start preparing for CAT. Why are you here?' I asked.

'Certainly not to buy this place,' she said and looked at Sidharth, who smirked. 'I am collecting brochures for my sister. It turns out she doesn't want to be what I want her to be; she wants to try out CAT, too. Let's see what happens.'

'Oh, your sister. She is out of rehab?'

'Yeah. It's been a while,' she said.

It was hard to believe six months had passed since I last saw her. Everything seemed like yesterday.

'Yes. Long time since we last talked.'

'You never called back,' she pointed out.

'I just got busy with stuff. I am sorry. Plus, I always thought Delhi is a small place and we would bump into each other. I didn't know it would take us six months!' I said. I couldn't help but notice that she looked even better now. Winter or no winter, the redness of her cheeks was permanent.

'If you are not doing anything, maybe we can catch a coffee later, after this?' she asked, her voice a little shaky.

I looked at Sidharth and he immediately said, 'Ohh, don't worry about me. I have *work* to do. Very important work. Like always. I will leave right now.'

It was apparent that he wasn't happy about me going out with her again, and at a certain level, I thought it was a bad idea, too. It took me six months and I still wasn't over her; she was trouble then, she could be trouble now. But then, turning down the prettiest girl in your life on a phone call is a different thing, and turning her down face-to-face is a different thing altogether. I wasn't up to the task.

***

'So she comes back from the dead?' I asked.

'Yes,' Joy said. 'Six months. Just when I was so over her, she made a comeback. And this time, she looked even better than before.'

'But it's commendable you held out for six months,' I said.

'Yeah. I know, but it wasn't easy—in fact, there wasn't a single day when I didn't feel like calling her and talking to her. But then, I had everything to lose and nothing to gain. Just the thought of her being with someone else was crushing.'

'So, why did you say yes to her when she asked you out in the coaching centre?' I asked him.

'Neeti?' he said. 'When I refer to her as the prettiest girl in the whole darn universe, I mean it! It's not an exaggeration, it's a plain fact. She is what I say she is; it's the gospel truth.'

'Okay, okay. I get it, stop making me feel ugly and hideous. So, what after that?'

'We went out to a café near the coaching centre,' he said. 'And . . .'

***

The First True and Everlasting Love—Part 4

'So where have you been these six months? What has been going on?' she asked. She ordered cappuccinos for both of us.

'Nothing really. The usual. College. Classes.'

'The last time you met me, you said you guys didn't attend classes anymore!'

'Now we do. Sidharth wants to go out for a year and study, and hence needs a stronger profile,' I said. 'What about you? How is your sister? All well now?'

'Yes. She responded well to the treatment and she is now all set to take charge of her life again. She wants to get back on track and so there I was—for her,' she smiled, and pumped her fist comically; she was still entertaining.

'Good for her. And are you still dating that guy? The smart, thoughtful guy who was intelligent, ambitious and focused?'

'I am surprised you remember! It's strange how we start to see people differently when we are with them. He is nothing of that sort. He is an enormous prick, jerk of the highest order. Oh, and we broke up. We were going through a rough patch when I met you, and it didn't last too long. I guess I broke up within a month or so after that,' she said.

'*Fuck!*' I said. I didn't want to say it aloud.

'What?' she said. 'What happened?'

'Oh! Nothing!'

'Tell me,' she said.

'You said you broke up with him within a month?' I asked, half-smiling and half-laughing; it was tragic and it was funny. It was tragic because all this time I was putting myself through death imagining her with a boyfriend, and it was funny because I am stupid as hell.

'Why? Yes. We broke up within a month, maybe fifteen days. Why? What's the matter? You are freaking me out, Joy.'

I couldn't stop smiling at the irony of the whole situation. If only I had picked up her calls, I would have probably known.

'You know why I *never* called you back?' I said.

'It would help me a lot, yes, especially now that you are smiling like a maniac!' she said, half-scared at my strange behaviour.

'Because I thought you had a boyfriend. And I didn't want to get into all this,' I said.

'So I had a boyfriend. What? And what *all this*? I am really not getting you. Stop talking in puzzles,' she said.

'Look, the thing is, Manika, I am sure that a lot of people have probably said this, but you are very pretty, smart too . . .'

'Thank you.'

'Shut up, I am not finished yet,' I said. 'See, you are very pretty, it's not even funny how pretty you are, and I don't know if you notice it but people stop what they are doing and stare at you, that's how pretty you are, but that's not why I like you so much. Well, like every boy I like good-looking girls, and they are my weakness, and I am not going to lie to you but I am a very vulnerable guy and fall in love pretty easily. But then, you're so smart and those eighteen hours that we spent together were so incredible! I couldn't stop thinking about them, and it might sound maniacal, but since then I have read every book you had talked about. EVERY. ONE. OF. THEM. And the funny part is that I like them, a LOT. And every time I used to think of you with someone else, I felt sick, like physically sick. I knew that I couldn't see you any longer, because I was sure that the more time I would spend with you, the more I would fall in love with you. So, I just stayed away.'

'But . . .'

'I saved my heart from breaking. So I am sorry, but I couldn't have answered your calls or be anywhere near you while knowing that you were with somebody else. It was just too much for me to take. I know it is creepy, Manika, but that's what it is like.'

'Hey, Joy,' she said. 'Look at me.' She tried to make eye contact, as I looked away, embarrassed and shy and almost crying.

'Yes?'

'That's the cutest thing anyone has *ever* said to me. I wouldn't deny that it was creepy in portions, but it was cute nonetheless!'

'Thank you,' I said.

'And,' she continued, 'you shouldn't have disappeared.'

'I am sorry for that.'

'Why did you think I called you so many times, you fool?'

'Umm . . .? No idea.'

'After I broke up with *him*, the supposedly smart and thoughtful guy, the only person I thought about was *you*. And it wasn't just you who had a great time that day, I had a wonderful time too!'

'You did?'

'Yes. You are almost the reason why I broke up with him,' she said.

'C'mon. Now you're kidding.'

'I am *not*. We were fighting since long, but after that day and that night with you, I realized that what I had with him was not what I wanted. I wanted more dates like the ones I had with you. I didn't know whether I wanted you or not, but I knew I didn't want him for sure. I thought about talking to you about it but you never called back. And then I just thought I was one of the many girls you date. I mean, you know, you are cute and I am sure a lot of girls would like to be with you,' she said.

'Believe me, no one, and I mean no one wants to be with me,' I said.

'Are you sure?' she asked with a wicked smile.

'Unless you want to be!' I beamed.

'Maybe,' she said, shyly.

'Can you say what all you just said one more time? I need to record it and play it every day for the rest of my life because I am sure it will never happen again,' I said and she laughed.

And then we both laughed, and we laughed till she had tears in her eyes, and it wasn't even funny. I kicked myself for staying away from her all these months, and I thanked Sidharth, Sidharth's dad, his mom, Aman, Vani and everybody who had caused the serendipity.

'Better late than never,' I said.

'Better late than never,' she said and smiled.

* * *

'Awww, that's so sweet,' I said as he grinned from ear to ear.

'You have no idea how happy I was after that. We went to her place after that.'

'Oye hoye!' I interrupted.

'Shut up, it's nothing like that. Nothing of that sort happened. And it still was pretty good. We didn't sleep all night. We just talked, stared at each other, asked each other things close to us and by the time I left her place, it seemed like I had never not known her. It felt like she had always been around. I never felt out of place, never an awkward moment of silence. It nearly broke my heart to leave her place in the morning, and she said she felt the same. It was like we had skipped the part where I should have pursued her, the part where she would have played hard-to-get and got straightaway to the part where we thought about why the hell we weren't together when we were so good together. It was insane. That night remains my best night ever. I never had smiled, laughed and felt quite so good . . . There was never a dull moment.'

'That's sweet. Yet boring. Skip that! So, when did you ask her out?'

'I didn't,' he said. 'She did.'

'What? Don't tell me!' I said.

112

'Okay. I won't.'

'No, no, no. I meant, tell me everything. When did she ask you out?'

'It had been a few weeks, maybe even a month, and we kept going on dates, and it was pretty obvious that we really liked each other. She lived in a flat all by herself near her workplace and I spent a lot of time there during that time, and a lot of time meant whatever time I had. Our goodbyes alone lasted a few hours. I just didn't seem to get enough of her, and and she used to say the same, though I doubted it because I was so much in love with her and she probably did not want to see me disappointed.'

'And that's how you fell for her?' I asked.

'With me, only after it has been weeks into a relationship do I realize whether I truly love a girl or not . . . but with her, I knew from the very beginning that it wasn't a fling or anything.'

'That you loved her?'

'Yes. Almost immediately, she became an obsession. I used to count hours and minutes until the next time I would get to see her, being with Manika was all that mattered. She was all that mattered.'

'And she? She loved you?' I asked.

'You seem to be very sceptical about her,' he said.

'No, it's just that this Manika character, she sounds like one of those strong-headed women who don't fall in love, for whom guys are just like another piece of furniture, and they can live without them,' I said, trying not to offend him.

'She was exactly like that. However, with me, she was different. Soon enough, she became my baby, and we made our own little world,' Joy said and continued with the story. He really loved this girl. He started to tell me about how her one-room *apartment was more of a library with a solitary bed and a couch and a study table, the open kitchen, the posters of her favourite movies on the walls, and how they spent hour after hour reading books together.*

The First True and Everlasting Love—Part 5

Three months had passed and we were still together, we were still very very much in love. So, what was special about *this* love that wasn't there in the first two? Or that didn't really happen in later ones too?

I had gone berserk.

We met *every day* for I found it hard to stay away from her; distance pained me. Nothing even came close to rivalling the time I spent with her. She was so perfect in everything she did. Be it how she always smelled or the way she tied her hair behind her head in a neat bun or when she used to wake up before me and caress my hair while I pretended to be asleep. It was *perfect*. We never ran out of things to do, she often used to take me to these book launches that only the authors and their families attended, and though I used to be reluctant at first, I started loving them eventually. She told me that the greatest joy of any author is to see the twinkling eyes of the reader whose life he or she has changed through mere words on paper.

I used to spend whatever little money I had on her. And *more*.

~

'Mom?' I asked.

'Yes, baba?'

'I was thinking I should join the JAVA course. It really helps during placement time.'

'Didn't you do it last month?'

'Umm . . . err . . . that . . . was the foundation course. This is the more advanced version. Everyone is doing it,' I lied.

'Fine, Joy, but I thought you weren't interested in computers.'

'Mom, you have to be multifaceted to get a good placement these days,' I said, 'By the way, I have to pay them *today*. It's eight thousand and the discount only lasts till today.'

'Fine Joy I will write a cheque. What's the name of the institute?'

'Mom! The discount is only on cash payments, they don't accept cheques,' I said.

'*Why?*'

'How am I supposed to know?' I said. 'Maybe it has something to do with saving tax!'

'Fine,' she said, counted and handed over eight thousand to me.

That money went into a handbag that Manika loved, and I got mauled by her when I told her how I got the money. I couldn't have lied to her! I kept joining dozens of fictional computer courses to fund my spending on her. Mom used to think I was getting serious about life. Yes, I was getting *serious* about my life, it being Manika.

Just one shy smile of hers used to make my day. The best part of being with her was that the initial rush and the excitement of a new relationship showed *no* signs of wearing out! We just couldn't get over telling each other how much we loved each other. We told each other how lucky we were to be in love! We did everything we would see other couples do and then say, 'That's so tacky! Gay.'

Manika was a great girl, a little intimidating, but that was what made her so special. Unlike what I had first surmised about her, she was incredibly cute at times. It was like dating a completely new person every day—every day I uncovered a new layer, a new side to her. I loved the mystery and the aura around her. Some days she was a taskmaster and the very next, she would be a little *kid*, but what didn't change was how attracted I was to her. Those seductive eyes of hers, the wet-hair look, the intentional brush of her hands against mine, the occasional nibble on my ear—still gave me the chills.

She was *everything* I ever wanted or needed. Her face was the first one I wanted to see in the morning, her voice the first sound, her hair brushing against my face, the first touch, her hand was the one I longed to hold, her stories were the only ones I was interested in, her smile was all what mattered. The twinkle in her eyes sparkled with a light that was beyond a thousand stars. I loved her to bits and beyond; it was almost as if everything else had stopped to matter.

'And what would you do to me?' she whispered in my ear seductively as we sat in a room full of people in a creative writing seminar.

Manika had always wanted to write a book, and she was writing one since very long; she wasn't making considerable progress though. She had renewed the effort after she met me, saying that she had finally found the male protagonist in her story—*ME*! Needless to say, it was very flattering.

These seminars were what she attended whenever she hit a writer's block, and since I couldn't stay away from her, I always tagged along. I could have gone to a funeral with her and still have had a good time (and that's morbid). This is how much I loved being around her. Plus, with Sidharth always being busy with his projects and experiments, she was the only person left that I ever wanted to be with.

Anyway, the reason why we were there at this seminar was that she was stuck at a sex scene.

'I am really bad at this verbalizing-sex thing. Why don't you just write what *we* do? That's awesome lovemaking, isn't it? Or you can write about your ex-boyfriends if you think they were better!' I said.

'Stop it!'

'Fine,' I grumbled.

'And anyway, what we do might just be a little too much for the readers to digest,' she winked. 'But whatever, say something. Help me in this. C'mon, just talk dirty!' she said a little too loudly than she intended and people around us looked back to see who had said it. Manika just smiled at me, almost threatening me with a look that told me that she would say it louder the next time.

'Okay,' I whispered. 'I will rip the clothes off you.'

'That's boring, Joy. Where are the details? The fun is in the *details!*' she whisper-shouted again.

'Okay. Fine, fine. Just keep the volume low,' I told her, though she was least bothered and still laughing. She was really having fun at my expense. 'I run my fingers down your neck as my lips are breathing down heavily on your nape. You look down with your dreamy eyes, with quivering pink lips and—'

'Quivering lips? My foot! It's *you* who has quivering lips!'

'Do you want me to shut up?' I feigned anger.

'Sorry, sorry. Go on.'

'So yes, quivering lips, and I hold you by your nape, my lips on your bare neck, my tongue on your skin, and I press you onto me, and your breasts are heavy against me as you dig your claws into me. My hands wander on your back and untie the straps of your dress and it slides down your body and my fingers caress your back and clench you and you gasp.'

'Go on,' she said, no longer smiling. She breathed heavily and her hand had crept up my thigh. I just hoped no one else saw or listened as her hands grazed and moved further up; my breathing shortened and quickened.

'You step out of your dress, your ripe breasts lay naked in front of me, as I lunge onto you and kiss you on the lips, long and deep, my hands all over you, pulling the last shreds of clothes off you, laying you down naked,' I paused to catch my breath.

She clenched her hand on my thigh harder and added, 'And I fight to get your shirt off you, and hastily unbuckle your belt and let your manhood free. Go on . . .' she breathed heavier.

'Our naked bodies collide, skin against skin, tongue against tongue, fire against fire, as I take you down. We fight for dominance, as you struggle beneath me, as I pin you down harder, and get deeper inside you as you moan and bite my neck just to keep yourself from screaming. I bite you back and you let go, letting out a huge scream.'

'And I beg you to fuck me harder,' she said under her now laboured breath.

'And I gladly oblige, against the wall, against the table, on the table, on the bed, I take you down. My back becomes a battlefield for your nails; your breasts become the same for my teeth.'

'Hey, Joy,' she said, as she lifted her hand from my thigh. 'We need to go,' she said seriously. 'Just follow me.'

And I did, like a puppy behind its master.

'Where?' I said as she walked in front me and frantically looked for a place.

'Here.' She pointed out the men's washroom.

***

'No, you didn't!' I said.

'Yes, indeed,' he said, nonchalantly.

'You made out in the men's washroom? That's gross even by your standards!'

'My standards? Stop making me out to be a dirty bastard. She suggested it, and frankly I really wasn't in a position to make a sound judgment at the time,' he said.

'So did she break out of her writers' block?'

'So much so, that her book had almost twice the number of intimate moments than what she had initially planned,' Joy winked. 'It was all testosterone and oestrogen from there on in the book! She was so embarrassed by the time she completed it that she thought twice before telling her parents about it. I have to say, a few scenes were quite explicit.'

'But you don't look the good-in-bed type!' I said.

'Take that back if you want me to continue my story!' Joy gasped.

'Just kidding! Why do guys take this so seriously?' I mocked.

'I don't actually. Maybe I really sucked at it, but she never told me so,' he said and continued.

***

The First True and Everlasting Love—Part 6

'Why can't guys have multiple orgasms?' she said and kissed me.

'And that is exactly why I prefer females in bed—multiple orgasms, sweet smelling hair, smooth skin and beautiful eyes! Aren't these enough reasons?'

'Oh, you just know what to say, not so much as to what you have to do,' she said and hugged me. This is how she usually taunted me about my inexperience in bed. Since I was her eighth boyfriend and she was only my third girl, she was *much* more experienced. She was older! What could I have done?

'It's not *funny* when you refer to all the other guys that you have been with,' I said, not pleased at all; just the mere fact that somebody else had touched her before, would send me into fits of frenzy, and there were eight guys!

'Whatever I may say, and I hate to say this, but you are by far the *best*!' she said.

'That's sweet. But then you are a writer. It's easy for you to say these things!' I said, though I had really fallen for those words again.

'Aww *baby*, that's just an occupational hazard of dating me,' she said. 'But fancy words or not, I *mean* it. You are awesome,' she said, rolling me over and nibbling at my ear and giggling. We were at it again, and like always it felt like a million explosions.

We lost count of days we had spent lying about idly at her place, reading books together, talking, trying out new recipes together, and spending hours after hours cuddling and watching our favourite shows and movies. She was in between jobs for a few months and it seemed we never got off the bed. We definitely never ever made it out of her apartment. It had become our own little world with books and food and love; it seemed we didn't *need* anything else. I had hated the kitchen before, but now I loved serving her horribly burnt food, early in the morning while she purred in her sleep. At least, I made brilliant coffee, and I have to say, she was a bit of an adoring-fan girl!

My mother was tired of my frequent night-outs at Sidharth's place, but she didn't complain a lot; she thought I was studying hard for my CAT exams.

One day while we were cuddling and had buried ourselves in each other's arms, we heard footsteps in the main hall; it seemed like I had forgotten to bolt the main door again.

'Hey! Man! You guys disgust me. Fuck. This room stinks!' Sidharth said, as he entered through the door.

'Sidharth! Would it break your knuckles to knock before you enter?' Manika exclaimed as she pulled the blanket over herself. 'You're HORRIBLE!'

'No, but it would surely *not* give me a chance to see you naked,' he chuckled.

'Fuck you, Sidharth,' I said.

'Oh shut up. I would rather do it with her,' he chuckled.

'Whatever,' I said.

'And why don't you guys pick up the phone, damn it! I have been calling all morning. I wanted to tell you guys something, but you just can't seem to keep your hands free! Perverts!'

'Look who's talking! We are trying to avoid you, asshole,' she muttered. 'Is that too hard to understand?'

'Back to you, unemployed journalist and failed writer and the one who snatched my best friend away from me!' he retorted.

'Don't say that, Sidharth,' I said and hugged her. 'Her book is going pretty well, trust me!'

'Yeah, yeah. I know all about the never-ending book, which has you as the main character. Call me when she manages to finish it within this century!'

'You told him about the book?' Manika asked me. She had asked me not to tell anyone until she finished it; she said it would jinx it.

'You are all he talks about, Manika. I don't remember the last time he talked about anything else. I just want to know what spells you have put on my innocent friend. I always knew you were bad for him!' he said and smirked.

'As if you talk about anything other than your stupid projects,' I defended.

'Shut up, you two,' Manika said. 'Stop fighting like a married couple. Get a life!'

'I have a life. It's you,' I said and kissed Manika.

'That's so *gay* and so *gross*. Anyway,' Sidharth said, 'I have to tell you guys something really serious.'

'For a change,' Manika smirked.

'Whatever. The thing is that I have taken a transfer. I *got* the scholarship! So I will do the next three semesters, and maybe even my Master's, in the most romantic city in the world, PARIS!' he said and threw his arms wide open, grinning widely.

'What?' I said, staring in disbelief. '*THAT'S AWESOME!* Really? Come here!'

We hugged and jumped and I congratulated him repeatedly. I was so freaking happy for him. Out of all the geeks and the nerds that infested our college, one of us won the scholarship. *My best buddy!* I felt like I had done it, like I was going to France, not him. For all the times we were thrown out of class, this was the sweetest revenge.

'So when do you leave?' Manika asked.

'I am leaving this coming Monday,' he said, his voice now solemn.

. . . And that's when we realized the gravity of the situation; it struck us that he could be gone for a year, maybe more. Yes, at a certain level, I was extremely happy about him because he had always wanted to go there and study for a while, travel a little, and do all sorts of crazy stuff that only he did, and get some respect back, but we never thought he would actually make it. Even when he was working night and day for this scholarship, we thought a moment would come when he would give it all up and join us. But he didn't. Manika told me a few times that he would really see it through, and I felt guilty, because even I, his best friend, really didn't believe he had it in him to go through with it. Eventually, I was so glad he actually did it.

We never thought he would really go!

And now that he was going, it just *sucked* balls. The moment he said it, it felt like he had always been around and now, suddenly, he just wouldn't be there to get me into trouble as he always did. Sidharth would never be a part of our plans. Manika and I had gotten Manika's sister interested in Sidharth and we had decided to set her up with him. We had imagined the four of us together!

'But then again, long-distance relationships do work sometimes,' Manika said out loud, trying to lighten up the mood. 'You two will still stick it out. There is too much love to be lost,' she winked.

'I will ignore the homosexual jibe you just took, Manika. But I am going to miss you guys. Yes, Manika, I will miss you too. IMAGINE,' he sighed.

'I never thought I would be saying this, and it pains me to say this, but I will miss you too,' Manika replied. 'Especially since you were such a central character in the book! Now who will be Joy's best friend in the book?'

'Shut up,' he said. 'I will still be the best friend. I will *always* be. And if you don't remember, let me remind you that you wouldn't be naked next to him if it wasn't for me and that rave I dragged him to.'

Sidharth was going away. It was almost like a break-up, just that he was a guy with hairy legs and a little paunch, but I loved him.

'Sidharth?' Manika said. 'You know what? None of us believed that you would actually make it. Not him. Not me. So now that you have, you deserve a big party from us.'

'You really thought I couldn't do it?' he asked in all seriousness.

'Nope,' we echoed.

'Heck—even *I* thought I couldn't do it!'

That night, we had a big party for him. We didn't invite very many people, but there was a lot of booze, and then, there was *us*. We didn't need anyone else. We drank (I had started drinking occasionally), ate and cried together, and we promised each other that we would remain the best of friends no matter how many miles separated us. Then, one by one, everyone puked, passed out and slept, leaving just Sidharth and me awake and in our senses.

'So, Paris, eh?' I said. 'French girls in short summer dresses, depressing winters, and lots of wine. I am really happy for you.'

'Thank you,' he said, wistfully.

'And what did your parents say about it?'

'They are pretty happy. They never thought I could do something like this. But it's somewhat sad that I have to go now. I mean, it's Delhi. I never imagined myself anywhere else. The roads, the girls, the food, nothing will ever match up to this . . .'

'*Fuck off.* I am sure you can't wait to land there with all those firang chicks all around.'

He laughed. 'Yeah, that's something I am looking forward to, but it wouldn't be fun without you.'

'Bastard.'

'You shouldn't be jealous, Joy. You have Manika. And you are great together. Generally people say this to a girl, but I am going to say this to you, because we know how weak-ass you are—I hope she doesn't break your heart.'

'Thank you.'

'I am seriously happy for you guys. You look so complete with your books and your favourite authors and your old movies. Remember when I was with Vani? I thought that was it, but then I see you guys and I say to myself every day . . . that *this* is it. I would kill for where you are,' he said.

'I always knew you had the hots for my girlfriend!' I joked.

'Not funny. But stick with her. You are great with her.'

'I intend to go nowhere else,' I said.

We talked for a little while, drank a little more and drifted off to sleep. Anyway, time took its course and the day of his departure to France came and went.

For a month at least thereafter, I would be sad because there was nobody to do guy stuff with, but then again, I had Manika to take care of me. So everything went back to being just fine; I learned to live without him. Though, to date, it's never been more than two days that Sidharth and I haven't talked, and that was good enough.

From the moment Sidharth left, my relationship started getting serious with every passing minute, and I kept asking myself questions as to whether I should take the next step or not. To me, I had no doubt in my mind that I would see this relationship to its very end. *I love you, what can possibly go wrong?*, I always told her.

'Joy?' Manika said. 'Do you think we can last?'

'Yes.'

'You mean, in the long run, you and me?' she asked again, as she laid her head on my shoulder.

The question was meaningless for I was sure about her; for the last few months, she was all I needed and pined for. I was there when she left for office; I was there when she came back after office, when she woke up with her hair in tangles, when she went to sleep in the *Winnie-the-Pooh* imprinted pyjamas, on her good days, on her bad days—we were together 24/7! We were pretty much living together. I saw no reason why I wouldn't be able to do the same for the next many lives, together.

'I am sure about it, Manika. You are all I need, it's like you are everything I wanted in a girl. I can't be happier. I have seen how complete I am with you. I just don't want to be without you now. I can't be.'

'That's so sweet. But tell me, just hypothetically, if you wake up someday and I am not there, I am just not there, what would you feel like?' she asked in all earnest, and my eyes welled up almost instantly, and I wanted to run away from the question and the possibility.

It was *not* an option.

'I will do anything just to get to you. Anything.'

'What if I die?' she asked and I saw tears sprouting in the corner of her eyes too.

'I will follow you,' I said, and she hugged me. I felt her tears wet my shirt. We were together. We were always meant to be. I had chosen her.

For life.

***

'Awww, that's so sweet,' I said and hugged him. He looked so sweet when he repeated the dialogues he had said. And really, I had never imagined him like this; I had always seen him as a heartless bastard. So, I told him, 'It's almost unbelievable that you can talk like that. It's unreal. Which girl wouldn't love it?'

'Thank you, Neeti. But then, it really was effortless with her, it wasn't as if I was trying to be sweet. I didn't have to think before speaking back then. No pretences. No lies. I just poured out whatever I felt like and she liked it that way,' he said, ever so cutely.

Awww, I just wanted to cuddle him so bad. It was actually a shock for me to see him lovelorn, an absolute romantic.

'So, what next?' I said. 'When did you two write the book? The first one?'

'Hmmm, actually she wrote it. Almost all of it, and it was early in the fourth year of my engineering that she completed the book. So if you don't like the book, you have to blame Manika and not me.'

'When did it get released?'

'After it got accepted, it took a few months to come out in the

130

market. I read the manuscript on our first anniversary. I had read it in parts but she hadn't let me read the whole thing,' Joy said. 'And that's another story.'

'Tell me,' I said and Joy continued.

The First Book

Six months passed since Sidharth had left and another semester ended. Just a year left for my engineering and things couldn't be better; I couldn't have asked for anything else and everything was just *perfect*. My grades went up in my third year as Manika made sure I studied, and arguing with her was the last thing I ever wanted to do. As the fourth year started, so did the placement season. Since I had done so well in the last year, I fancied my chances in firms that I wouldn't have had a chance at, a year earlier.

'Are you nervous?' she asked as she ruffled my hair.

'What do you think?' I countered. I was freaking out, I was nervous and sweating and I felt like I would faint; the suit and the tie I wore were suffocating me and I wanted to run away. I could hear my heart pound ferociously.

'A little, maybe.'

'I am so glad you're with me today, I would have pissed in my pants out of nervousness. At least when I screw up the interview inside, I can come outside and feel lucky that I still have you,' I said.

'You're just being sweet!'

'I am not! Look around you, every guy is staring at you. They want you, and that's because you are gorgeous, they don't even know yet what a wonderful person you are. Every one of them should be nervous about the interview, but they are busy staring at you. You are what everyone wants. And I already have you! I think I have no reason to be nervous. I already have what I want the most,' I said.

'Joy, baby,' she said. 'Two things. One, sometimes, you make absolutely no sense.'

'Second?'

'That I am your girlfriend now. You really don't have to flirt with me like ALL THE TIME. By the way, you look like a pretty boy in a suit. Very nice, very smooth,' she said and I blushed.

We laughed and she wished me luck again, and then we made plans to visit the bookstore and pick up a box set of our favourite author, John Green.

'JOY!' the guy from the company called out.

'Hey. Interview time. Wish me luck,' I said.

'Best of luck,' she said and straightened my tie. 'Are you really going to leave me outside with all these guys in suits? Some of them are really handsome.'

'That's why I flirt, just to remind you that I am better than these nerds in suits. But, seriously, don't look at them because some of them are indeed handsome.'

'Enough. Now GO!' she smiled and blew me a kiss.

Everyone who saw that probably died of envy right there, twice. *Yes, she is mine!* My face screamed at them, as I strode inside the room for the interview with a big smile on my face.

A job well begun is half done. And talking of the job, I got it. I had prepared my resume well, Manika had made me practise talking about thirty seconds on every line of my resume, and the kind interviewer didn't ask me anything beyond my resume; I was confident and spot on. It was a good day. Being placed on the first day of placements, and a lot many people seeing that I was dating the girl of everyone's dreams is stuff legends are made of; that's how victory is spelled. I had *reasons* to celebrate. I was with Manika and that itself was a reason to celebrate every day.

'So,' she said, as we sat in the car. 'Where do we go today?'

'Can we just walk around the campus and show everyone that I am dating you. Because I think some people haven't seen you, and they really need to see you.'

'Someone has really been practising his lines,' she said.

'I stayed up all night to perfect these! And I also watch you sleep and stuff,' I said.

'Aw. So where do we go?'

'Hmmm,' I said. 'Why don't we do something *different* like going to your place, snuggling in with a book, and then maybe we can make out a little?'

'C'mon, that's what we always do!'

'That was *the* joke, Manika,' I said and we laughed out. 'Hey, wait. Mom is calling, I haven't told her about the interview yet. Shit.'

It was Mom, Dad and Di (my elder sister, the favourite child), everyone all at once. I lived with them, but usually three out of seven days, I lived with Manika. Mom had been furious about this for a long time, but when my grades improved, she patted my back and said she had no problem whatsoever with my study nights at my *friend's* place. She really believed that all those red marks on my neck were nothing but mosquito bites, or at least that's what she made me believe. Dad and Di always knew there was something fishy about the frequent night-outs and the strange marks on my neck, but they never said anything.

'What did she say?' she asked as soon as I disconnected the line.

'She wants me to come home. Celebrate with them.' As soon as I said this, her face fell and before she thought I could see that, she put a fake smile on.

'You should go, you should celebrate with them,' she said. 'I will drop you home. Probably we will celebrate it tomorrow? Fine?'

'No. Not fine. We will celebrate it today.'

'But Joy—'

'Never mind. Come with me, we will find a way out,' I said.

'*What?* Where?'

'Home. Where else?'

'Oh no, no, no. I am not coming. I am not even dressed properly,' she said.

'C'mon, you always look great! Just come!' I begged. 'They will love you!'

'And what are you going to introduce me as?'

'I will tell them the truth that we are married and you're expecting my child. In fact, twins, a boy and a girl,' I said with a straight face.

'What!'

'As a friend, Manika, what else?' I said.

'C'mon, they are your parents. They will *know* I am not just a friend. You will just be inviting trouble,' she said.

She was probably right. I was inviting trouble. If not anyone else, my mom would have certainly freaked out; in the past twenty-odd years I have never got a girlfriend home; she would have smelled trouble. It was already getting dark and taking a girl home this late was really the last thing I ought to do.

'Okay then. I will go,' I said. 'But I will come back. I will sit with them for a little while and then come back again. It will not take more than twenty minutes, I promise.'

'But—' she began to protest.

'Nothing doing. I want to be with you tonight and we will do something crazy! And I will see to it that it happens.'

We didn't discuss anything further. On our way, I thought about a million pretexts that would work out for *why* I wanted to leave the house so late at night even though I was already placed. *Another study session? In between placement week?* It was a little too much to digest. Mom would see through it. After my periodic absences for the last several months, I couldn't have told them that I was going out with my friends again.

What really troubled me was that this very day, one year back, Manika and I had first met at that party at the farmhouse. I really wanted to be with her. For me, the day we first met should have been our anniversary, though she thought differently because it wasn't until several months later that I asked her out, and we started dating properly, like a couple. I never bought that argument; I loved that night, the serendipity, and the mystery of the nameless girl with a cigarette dangling from her lips.

I had saved for the last three months and got her a watch engraved with her name and I really wanted to give it to her that day. I wanted to write something for her, but had got busy with the placements and couldn't. I really hoped she would like it.

'Hi! Congratulations!' Di said as soon as I entered the house.

Mom and Dad followed suit, hugged me and said they were proud of me. It was especially shocking for them, since they been to my college a couple of times to solve my attendance issues with my professors. So they never really had very high hopes from me. But now that I had proven them wrong, I felt happy about it. Not as much for myself as for *them*.

I am a guy and act like guys do. I don't tell my parents how my days go, I don't ask about theirs, I don't call them like my sister does, I forget their birthdays and Father's Day and Mother's Day, and my longest conversation with them is about money or food. But that doesn't mean I don't care, or I don't love them, I equally want to make them happy. I do it by talking about cricket and scoring well in my exams.

I was happy that day to see the glint in their eyes when I told them about the job. I had done them proud, and I hoped it made up for all the times they had just wanted to sit and talk to me but I watched television instead. Somehow, I find it hard to tell my parents that I love them; I think that's my weakness, or our weakness, and usually we need a foreign internship or a nice job to express it.

Anyway, my mind was still stuck on Manika, who was waiting in the car.

'So, where are they going to place you?' Mom asked.

'I don't know that yet,' I said. 'I still haven't gone through the offer letter.'

'Please tell them that you won't go out of Delhi. You anyway don't eat anything. God knows what will happen if they send you somewhere else!' Mom said.

We all laughed at this.

After a few more questions from Dad about the job profile and the company, Mom motioned us towards the dining table; the chicken smelled delicious. Even though it was very tempting, I was in no mood to eat.

'Di,' I whispered.

'What?' she said. 'And why are you whispering?'

'Manika is waiting. I need an excuse to run. What do I say?' I asked her. 'It's our anniversary, I just HAVE to go.'

'What? Mom will not let you go! It's already too late.'

'Do something. She is waiting in the car,' I begged.

'Fine,' she said.

I thought she would concoct a serious sounding story and narrate it to Mom, but instead she went up to Dad and told him *everything*. As I stood there, nervously watching and waiting for Mom to serve dinner, a smile broke out on Dad's face.

As we sat down to eat, Dad looked at me and said, 'Joy, Sumit called. He said your phone was not reachable? Some symposium or presentation you had to make together?'

'Symposium?' I asked, puzzled. And it was only when Di shot across a *how–dumb–you–are* look, did I realize what was going on.

'The *symposium*!' Dad said. 'He said something about IIT Delhi and some competition. I don't really remember!'

'What?' Mom asked as soon as she heard IIT; she had always dreamt of me going to IIT. She used to get very excited at the very mention of the name of the institute.

'Oh, Mom. It's a symposium that we had to attend. A paper presentation competition. We were in the final three and the competition is tomorrow. But we haven't prepared really, so there's no point going there now,' I said, as Di and Dad silently chuckled.

'*Why?* Why not? You should go.' Mom said. 'You have the whole night to prepare.'

'But . . .'

'Look, we can celebrate tomorrow. You eat now, and you can go over to his place and finish the presentation? Just because you're placed doesn't mean you will stop studying,' Mom looked at Di and Dad, and they nodded furiously, trying not to smile. I ate like a madman and rushed like one downstairs. I heard Mom praise me for what a *hardworking* kid I was.

Manika was still waiting in the car, her seat pushed back, music blaring out of her car's speakers, and she was reading a book we bought on our way back from college to my place. She sat up and smiled as soon as she saw me.

'Twenty minutes, exact!' she said. 'Not bad! What did you tell them?'

'Nothing. Oh yes, Mom packed this for you . . . or for Sumit, whosoever's house I am going tonight. I have to prepare for the symposium tomorrow at IIT Delhi.'

'Oh, so I am Sumit today,' she smiled.

'I must say Sumit suffers from a real bad case of male boobs.'

'Very funny,' she said. 'And you have eaten?'

'Yes. I have. Do you think she would have let me leave without eating? Bengali moms are crazy about kids not eating, but I can eat a little more. I think there is plenty for us in here.'

'Okay then, let's drop everything else and do something *different* as you said. Let's hang out at my place,' she said and laughed. 'Anyway, it's been a tiring day, hasn't it?'

'Yep,' I said as I clutched my bag. The watch was still there. I thought it was beautiful and corny and lovely. I hoped she would like it too. She drove and we talked about the possibility of where my job might take me, and she assured me she would find a job wherever I was posted. I was starting to feel a little bad that she *didn't* remember our anniversary, the day we first met.

'So, here we are,' she said, as she flopped on the couch. 'Come to me, my corporate hot shot!'

It really was a tiring day. The written exams, the four rounds of interviews, it really was a long day and it had taken a lot out of us. We had been at the college since the morning and I had spent eight hours bound in that horrible suit.

I didn't know when to give the watch to her, but then I thought I should get it out of the way soon.

'What time is it?' I asked.

'I don't know,' she said. 'You know I don't wear a watch.'

'Seems like it's time to start wearing one,' I said and dangled the watch in front of her, almost like a dead rat, very unromantically.

'Oh, it's for me?' she said and hugged me as I sat next to her. 'Awww, this is beautiful! This is so beautiful. Thank you!'

'Turn it around.'

She did and read the inscription aloud, '*To Manika, Joy. To our timeless, limitless love.*'

'This is so sweet! This is so sweet! A little creepy, but very sweet!' she said as she ran her finger over the inscription and then kissed me. '*Happy Anniversary*, baby Joy.'

'What?' I said. 'You remember?'

'Yes, I do. Obviously I do, dumbass. I am a girl. Even if I try, I can't forget these things!' she said.

'So you remembered and still didn't get me anything? How mean!' I said, playfully. 'And you're the older one!'

'You selfish bastard.'

'I am just kidding,' I said, as I pulled her towards me. '*You* are my gift! All wrapped around. Let me unwrap you! What say?'

She broke out of my embrace and said, 'That's for later, you desperate boy. For now, let me get you the real gift. Yes, I did get you something,' she said and went inside and returned with two gift-wrapped boxes.

'Open this,' she said and passed on the first one, and I opened the tore the gift wrap and pried open the box.

'C'mon! C'mon! This is not fair? *A Tissot?* This looks so expensive! Fuck, it's awesome. But now, my gift looks so cheap and inexpensive and sad. This is not fair! Why did you have to spoil my gift!' I said.

'I would take a plastic watch with an engraved inscription any day, rather than the one you are holding in your hands,' she said. And she said it with so much love in her voice that I really felt bad about saying what I had.

'So, I win?' I asked.

'Yes,' she said and kissed me on the forehead. 'Like always.'

'What's the other gift?' I asked.

'It's something you have been asking me to do for a really long time. So, I finally decided I would give you that today. Please be kind.'

'What? *Sex?* But we have already done that, haven't we?' I joked.

'Nope. *This,*' she said and handed over the next box, even more intricately wrapped than the first one.

I opened the box and inside it was the completed manuscript of her book, printed paper spiral bound in black plastic, the book I had been asking her to complete for a long time, since she said she would only let me read it when she completed it. The book was the only thing she spent more time on than me, and I had started to envy the book and the sheets of paper she ran her slender fingers on; she had struggled with her book for quite some time now, but it now lay completed in my hands. I was happy for her.

'Let's read this tonight,' I said, smiling. I couldn't wait to read and see what my character was like! She was right. Maybe the inscription on the watch held more value than the watch itself, just like her completed manuscript did for me.

'Don't you think we have better things to do tonight?' she said and whispered in my ear, her breath on mine, and her hand slipping inside my shirt, 'Happy Anniversary.'

'Happy Anniversary!' I said, already turned on.

'Hey, hey, hey,' she said as she pushed me away. 'I have something else, too. Wait.'

'What? I don't want anything else! You have already done enough! Just come here.'

'Give me two minutes,' she said, smiled wickedly, went inside the bedroom, and bolted it from the inside. I waited and tried to stabilize my breathing, which had shot through the roof now.

'Okay. I am coming out now. Even if you don't like it, just say that you do! I can take lies,' she shouted.

'I like everything about you,' I shouted back.

And then she came out. I suppressed a smile; I didn't know whether to smile or feel seduced. Manika since long had had eyes on a satin night thing—a *very* skimpy spaghetti and matching pink hot pants or whatever they are called. Her fulsome cleavage peeked out of the spaghetti and her legs were barely covered. She was looking freakishly inviting but then, it was funny at certain levels too. She didn't have to *try* to look hot. She was that anyway, but now that she tried, it was just not her.

'Joy huh! You are not supposed to smile!' she said.

'I am not!' I said. 'It's very hot. I mean, *very* hot.'

It was. Like. Totally. Hot. She stood a few yards away from me, hands on her waist and ass protruding, like a teacup, only thinner and alive and gorgeous. I couldn't keep my eyes off her cleavage and her legs. I mentally ran my hands over every part of her porcelain skin.

'Thank you,' I said.

'Like it?' she asked.

'I love it, baby,' I said. 'Even though I have always hated clothes on you, this is *hot*. I can make an exception today.'

Her ensemble didn't last on her too long, for soon it on the floor and she was on me. Though, I might have smiled when she first wore it, ever since that day, I pressured her to wear it every day that I was her place. We even got two more of them: one in red and another in white. *It was the best anniversary gift ever*, Satin Camisole and Hot Pants (that's what they are called—she told me later).

Heaven.

~

'It's freaking out of this world, Manika,' I exclaimed.

In my hand lay her first book—*Life. Served Hot*. It was ninety thousand words of pure delight and I had read it in one go, and then I had read it *twice*. It was better than the sex we had had the previous night, and that's like the best review she will ever get for the manuscript.

I don't say this because she was my girlfriend but because it was pure magic. Immediately after putting the phone down, I browsed through my favourite scenes again; one amongst them being the sex scene that we had written jointly. It wasn't all that bad. I patted myself.

It had been a month since she had completed it, but she didn't want me to read it until the day before. She wanted our anniversary to be special and special it was. Though I had to think of a reason for Mom as to where that expensive watch came from, it turned out to be rather easy to convince her—we had won the competition at IIT Delhi.

Anyway, Manika had been really nervous and said that I

shouldn't read it in front of her so I had gone back home the next morning and had read it. But now that I read it, I saw no reason why she should have been nervous. It was *fabulous*! I couldn't wait to meet her. She had told me the previous day that a small independent publisher had shown interest in the book and had asked her to come back to them whenever she finished it. She wanted me to read it before she contacted them again.

'I think you should meet the publishers,' I said, as I entered her place. 'It's awesome!'

'But it's nothing like what we are used to reading and you know that. I am so disappointed in myself. This book is trash! I don't really feel like getting it published.'

'Manika? I have read it twice! It's awesome! And it's not like every book has to be of the same type and cater to the same people. When literary authors write books, they know the kind of people who will read it, when commercial authors write, they know their audience too. It's not about who's better and who's not, they are just *different*.'

'What if they don't like it? Even I don't like it. And you will obviously like it, you're my boyfriend.'

'They would! And what's the harm in meeting them?'

She kept saying no, but I kept insisting. An hour later, we were outside the publisher's office.

'I am nervous,' she said as we stood at the gate of Bramha Publishers and Distributors. I had never seen her so low on confidence.

'Don't worry. You know it's awesome. They know it's awesome and that's why they have called you here. Plus, if I were a publisher, I would have just put you on my publishing list just because you are so freaking beautiful! That's got to count too, right,' I kissed her.

'Stop it,' she said, as we entered the premises and a very polite gentleman led us to the office of the owner of the publishing house.

'Hi. I am Soumitra,' he said, a man of nearly fifty-five with a disarming smile, and shook our hands. 'You must be Manika . . . and you are?'

'I am a friend of hers,' I answered

'Take a seat, please,' he said. A few more pleasantries later, he came to the point. 'Manika, it's beyond doubt the best manuscript I have read in recent years. We were looking for a book that fits our mass market publishing list and your manuscript it perfect for it. I usually don't read the manuscripts that are submitted, the editors do, but this time, they asked me go through it for they certainly see potential in this one.'

I looked at her. Manika was smiling. She had taken an instant liking to this man.

'Thank you, sir,' she said, almost a little embarrassed at the unabashed praise.

'You don't have to thank me for it! I am sure I will be the one thanking you when this book hits the bestseller charts,' he said and fished for something in the drawer. 'Here. We have drawn up a contract for you and you can go through it. If you like it, we would be ecstatic to have you here at Bramha Publications.'

He smiled and Manika looked at me. It almost seemed like she would have signed it right there and then. But she paused and there was an awkward silence.

'Hey,' Soumitra said and smiled again at us. 'Take your time. We are in no hurry! Take this home, review it and then let us know.'

'Thank you, sir,' Manika gushed. 'We will certainly do that.'

It was probably the first time that I had seen Manika being indecisive, because she was usually the one taking charge and kicking butt.

'Anyway, let's keep this aside and talk about your book,' he said.

'Sure, sir,' she said, her confidence and authority creeping back in her voice now that it was her territory.

'You have written it from a guy's perspective and it is brilliant. But why did you do it? I mean, as a reader, I would feel strange if a female author tries to write a guy's point of view. Because after all, you know the readers' psyche, right? They think the story is autobiographical, as most first books are, and that the story is about the author. They forget that its fiction and they start to think that the character is the author itself,' he said.

He had a point. If you read any book, especially from debutant authors, the *author* is the *character*, and more often than not, it's true. No two ways about it. At least, I have always felt that.

'Yes, I agree with you, sir, but I had to write from a guy's perspective because it is certainly most interesting to try and second guess how they think. Every girl thinks differently, but guys . . . they are like a herd, they think alike, they talk alike, they walk alike . . . you get the drift,' she said, not making any sense.

'I am sure your friend here doesn't agree to you calling him a part of the herd,' Soumitra mischievously smiled and looked at me. He had spotted my discomfort at her inconsiderate generalization.

Thereafter, Soumitra and Manika talked about books, and her influences and how she came about writing, and after a little while, we left the office with jubilant handshakes and congratulatory messages exchanged all around. He said he would be sending her a few rudimentary cover page ideas by the evening.

'So, what do you think? You are going to sign up with them?'

'Umm.'

'He seems like a nice man and he really likes your book,' I said, as we moved out of their office.

'He is. But I was thinking about something else,' she said, as she unlocked the car.

'What?'

She held my hand and came near, 'I think you should get credit for the book. Be a co-author.'

'*What*?'

'What *what*? It's simple. Put your name on the cover and everybody will think the main character is *you*. And his love interest is me. And it's fair, too, because parts of it are inspired by us. Anyway, a lot of story ideas came from you.'

'But . . .'

'And had you not pushed me and believed in me, I would have never finished this. It's only because of you that I was able to finish this,' she argued.

'*No*. Firstly, it's not fair because I haven't written it. Secondly, I don't want to snatch away your thunder. It's your book, and it's only fair that your name goes up there, not mine,' I said.

'Joy, I don't want anything that doesn't have you in it. It's meaningless. This,' she pointed to the contract, 'means nothing without you. I will not go ahead with this if this doesn't include you.'

What could I have said? I just hugged her and said we would talk about it, and she said that there was nothing to talk about. A zillion such arguments and a million such fights later, we signed the contract *together* for *Life. Served Hot.* The book cover would have both our names; we even split the royalty halfway! She said it was the good boyfriend premium. I didn't fight. You don't fight over and over again with a girl half as beautiful as her.

As soon as we signed the contract, everything was put into fast forward mode. Soumitra put the best of his editorial and designing team behind us and we worked nights together to finalize the book; the cover was a beautiful white and red with coffee cups and flowers. In four months we had the first copy of the book in our hands; they had done this book as a crunch-time book.

It was Manika's first book, our first book, a copyright that would stay with us for the next hundred years. The book released across bookstores all around the country on the fourth of August; we knew nothing about how our lives were to change, a little bit every day, since that day in August.

'This looks nice, doesn't it?' Manika said.

'It does. Now you have something to say to your grandchildren,' I said. 'They gave you a pretty generous print run too.'

'I don't care how many people read this book. If someone comes up to me and takes all of this away,' she waved the book 'and gives me one extra day to spend with you like this, I would be the happiest person to give it all away.'

'And I will go and find that *someone*, snatch the book and give it back to you! After all, who's he to give you one extra day with me? I am not going anywhere.'

'Not even when your mom lines up cute Bengali females in front of you with huge cash balances, big cars and big eyes?'

'Nope. Not a chance in hell!'

'I have heard Bengali women are great in bed!' she said.

'Are you trying to push me away? And no! Not even then.'

'Not even if the girls have personal villas on the beaches of France?'

'You are everything to me,' I said.

'As if I was letting you go anywhere,' she said, smiled and hugged me tight. 'I was just testing you.'

She closed her eyes, smiled at me and slept with her head on my shoulder. *Finest day of my life.*

***

'Oh. I loved that book!' I exclaimed. 'Well, not really. It was amateurish at best, but it had its moments!'

'Aha! Which book?' Joy smirked. 'It's a fictional book I am talking about. Why do you forget that I am just telling you a story and none of this really exists?'

'Oh, yes. This is just a story. Manika is fictional. The book that the two of you wrote in the story is fictional,' I laughed.

I let him play his little game. I knew who Manika was. I knew that the book was not named Life. Served Hot—it had a long and corny title, but I played along. It was, after all, an interesting story, fictional or not.

'True, none of this exists,' Joy said.

'So your life changed? How?' I asked. 'Facebook requests? People asking if you were the main guy in the book?'

'Precisely. And a lot of female attention,' he said. 'Something that I wasn't used to. AT. ALL.'

I remember how his social networking profiles exploded with people. People younger than him started addressing him as Sir in wall posts and scraps and it was really funny, because to me he was still a dumb dickhead. I remember blocking his posts from my wall, since there were just so many of them!

'Yes, I noticed,' I said. 'And that's when you started ignoring *all of us.'*

'Awww, I never ignored you!'

'Oh, you did!' I protested.

'Shut up,' he said. 'And it was just that too many things were happening at the same time. The book came out and my college ended six months later, and I had to join my office and Manika and I had just completed two years. I was really caught up with stuff.'

'No other notable thing happened in the period?' I asked.

'Other than the book—nope. We were still very much in love! And still very much together.'

'Two years, then huh?' I said. 'So did you do anything special on your second anniversary?'

'I gave her a ring this time. Without an inscription though. And she gave me a huge handmade card and a PlayStation.'

'That's cute.'

'I know,' he said.

'Okay, fine. Continue . Oh, didn't Sidharth come back?'

'Naah, after his engineering, he decided to stay back in Paris to complete his Master's from there. Although he was touring all over Europe, visiting strip clubs and God knows what. Anyway, where were we?' he asked. 'Oh the book, yes. The book was read by slightly more than the ten people we thought would read it. It was a shocker.'

***

The Change

'*Hindustan Times*. *The Hindu*. That's *The Telegraph*. And *India Today*. All this month!' Soumitra said, as he slipped the newspaper cuttings one by one in front of us.

Life. Served Hot made it to a few bestseller lists that mattered, and it had been just a few months past its release. We wondered if it was our publisher's PR stunt; there was no way so many people were reading our book.

Slowly and steadily, people started adding us and following us on social networks; all of them had questions about our book and we gladly answered them. There were a few nasty reviews too, but I tried to keep Manika as far away as I could from them.

The main characters in the book, Deboshree and Avik, were thought to be real people. And most of the mails were addressed to me as Avik, the male character in the book, and the mails to her as Deboshree, the female character of the book. It was *crazy*! Although I really liked the book (and Manika hated it), we didn't guess so many people would read it, and enjoy it. We had expected the book to go out of print in a short span of time but it was working so damn well. It was beyond my expectations.

As the book started being recognized, I started handling the conversations with our publisher, Soumitra; Manika was strangely detached from the book and the attention it got. She wasn't ever bothered about the readers, or the reviews, or how much it sold.

We were in love and that's what we cared about, life hadn't changed at all, she was still buried in her thick books and journals; she started working on her second book, and this time she pulled me in for a more central role, reading every chapter as she wrote it, tagging comments, editing and rewriting stuff. It was getting very exciting. A few days later, we got our first royalty cheques and we were ecstatic. My parents were first shocked and taken aback, and then proud, and then confused and they didn't know what to say.

It wasn't as if we became overnight celebrities. Still, no one really knew us, but I wasn't used to attention and I enjoyed whatever little I would get. Manika had always been against adding readers on Facebook, citing privacy as a reason. I, however, was never against it and soon there were a lot of people on my social networking profiles; it was crazy.

~

We got home that day from our publisher's office and we were smiling.

'Crazy, right?' she said, as she hugged me closer.

'I know, baby. It's bigger than what we had ever expected. I told you, more than ten people will read this book!'

'I still don't see a reason why people would want to read this book. But see how happy you are? And to think about it, you never wanted to be a part of it!' she kissed me.

'It's all because of you, baby,' I kissed her back.

'Aww!'

I often wondered how dispassionate she was about the success of the book. Manika always acted as if it meant nothing to her. She was still firmly grounded. She didn't even seem happy! She was just as she was before.

'So what do you think, continuing with the same characters in the next book will do the trick?' I asked her.

'I think so. I mean, that's what I want to write, it's up to the publishers whether they like it or not,' she said.

'Every day I get a few questions asking about our *next* book!'

'Don't worry. Public memory is short and they will soon forget us. There are better books and better authors to be read. Will you still love me when we are not famous?' she chuckled.

'Very funny.'

'Joy, I was fantasizing yesterday about turning into a full-time author, subject to the condition that I start writing better books. I can actually give up everything and do just that. No jobs, nothing, just you and me, lying in this bed, writing and reading books. Wouldn't that be ideal?'

'It's a nice thought, but I need to go,' I said, as I got up from the bed. 'My office is really getting hectic and every time I slip up there, they just ask me to *go, write a book!*' I said and pulled up my tie. 'And do finish that chapter, baby. Soumitra has been asking about the progress. And you know I can't write it as well as you do. Not in my wildest dreams!'

'It's strange. Only yesterday, you were just a little college boy, and today, you are a writer and an engineer. Times change,' she said as she pulled the pillow over her head.

'Funny!' I said and kissed her goodbye. 'But please, do finish the chapter, it's really important. He has asked for it many times now!'

She didn't seem to hear and went back to sleep in her tiny satin hot pants. I wanted to slip into bed with her, too. Her glistening legs were an awesome temptation, but I had things to do, and places to go.

The new office I had joined sucked. There was too much pressure and politics, and I never liked being around a bunch of mechanical engineers discussing thermodynamics and pipe stresses; it bored me and made me feel worthless. I used to spend hours staring at my computer screen and daydream about the possibilities that lay in front of us. I was becoming obsessed with what could and would be.

Last heard, John Green was working on a book that I felt would be epic. True, he was the Tom Cruise and Brad Pitt of fiction all rolled in one and I was Jugal Hansraj at best, but who cared as long as we were writing and we enjoyed it.

~

'Joy?' Manika said.

'Yes.'

'Who is Chhavi?'

'Chhavi who?' I asked.

'Chhavi Singh?'

'Oh. Facebook. She is just a reader. She is fascinated by our book.'

'*Just* a reader?' she sounded a little pissed. 'She has written in a post that you called her *edible*.'

'Me? Oh, that's was more like, she called me edible and I said, same to you or something like that.'

'You chatted with her? Like online?'

'Yes, I did. Just generally. She had some questions and I answered them.'

'Just generally? There were about forty messages between you and her in your FB inbox,' she said, accusingly.

'So? It was just usual conversation. It's nothing that you should be worried about. You must have read it.'

'Yes, and you were flirting with her.'

'It meant nothing,' I said. 'Just light-hearted conversation, baby!'

'Fine,' Manika said and buried herself in the book she was reading earlier, a thick book which looked new and I didn't remember when she had bought it.

Not again, I said to myself. She looked upset. I went up to her and sat beside her. I took her hand in mine and rolled her over; her eyes were teary.

'What happened, baby?' I asked her and ran my hand over her face.

'Nothing,' she said.

'Tell me,' I said and kissed her on the forehead.

'It's just that I don't like you like this. I loved the old Joy better.'

'I am still the same. Nothing has changed, baby.'

'It has. You have. Now you are always busy with either your office, or the book. If not that, you are always on Facebook or Twitter. It sucks. Where did *my* Joy go? Who did nothing but lie around in bed and sleep,' she smiled beneath her tears.

'I am still the same, baby. But I can't skip work. You know that.'

'But you can skip the other things, right?' she asked.

'But . . .' I really had nothing to say.

'It's okay,' she said and hugged me. 'You must be getting late. Now hurry. I will see you in the evening. 'Your mom won't ask you to come home?' she asked.

'I have told her that I'll be staying at a friend's place for most of the days. She knows it takes two hours to get from office from my place,' I explained. 'I should shift in here soon. I love you.'

'I love you too, Joy.'

I kissed her and left. She wasn't home when I came back. When she returned late that night, I had already fallen asleep by the time she got back.

Over the next few months, I started to spend a lot of time on Facebook, chatting and talking to people, replying to mails and messages, and this only meant more trouble, more fights and more tears.

***

'You were changing,' I said, already feeling a little bad about Manika.

'Yes, I was, I realize that now.'

'Bastard,' I said. 'Why are all guys like this? You two were so good together, like perfect.'

As he narrated the previous portion, all the love had drained from his voice. It reeked of foolish ambition, recklessness and lofty dreams. He no longer sounded like the lovestruck, picture-perfect boyfriend. And within my heart, I had started hating Joy a little. After all those promises and dreams . . . how could Joy be . . .?

'So what did you do next? Break up with her?' I asked.

'Yes,' he said. 'Actually she broke up with me, but I gave her the reason. Reasons, in fact, loads of them.'

'But the second book still came out, right? You must be really happy with that. That's what you wanted, didn't you? Just that the two of you write together?' I asked angrily, just to clarify things. Maybe even to needle him. Frankly speaking, I was so angry with him at this point that I didn't really care what he had to say. How could he have done it? He was so much in love with her! Or at least that's what he had said. All men are bastards. Joy was no different; he had cheated on her. I waited

158

patiently to see if his story would give any justification for what he did to her.

'It sure did,' he said. 'But . . .' Joy continued his narration.

The Second Book

'What about *Life, the Second Serving?*' Manika asked.

'It's brilliant,' Soumitra said. 'So when do you plan to release it?'

'Before the Kolkata Book Fair,' I said.

'That's exactly what I was thinking,' he said and slipped the contract papers in front of us. I signed it and passed it on to Manika. She had not said or addressed a word to me in the last one hour that we were sitting there. She was colder than the coldest day of winter and I hated it.

'I have my own pen,' she said, signed the contract and passed it on to Soumitra.

I went over the finer details of the cover design and the editing and the timelines of the book. Manika just sat there texting on her cell phone. She was least interested in what we were doing; it was irritating. As soon as we left the office, she started walking towards her car. It had been exactly one year that we had walked out of that office with huge grins on our faces. This day was starkly *different*.

'*Manika?*' I shouted behind her back.

She looked back.

'What?' she said as I walked up to her.

'Can we talk at least? Look, I am sor—'

'No, we can't.'

'But—'

'Joy, we could have talked before you decided to cheat on me! We could have talked then, not now. NOT NOW! Go to hell, Joy'

'Manika, I didn't mean to.'

'What, Joy? You lied to me! You fucking lied to me on my face, Joy!'

'I . . . uhh . . .'

'There is nothing you can say to make this better. This was the last fucking thing we'll do together. We signed it. And from now on, you go your own way, and I go mine. I hope this is the last time I see you,' she said and turned around.

'But we can still be in touch—'

'Is it? Is that what you *want*? I don't think so, Joy. You got what you wanted—another book. Now go on, have as many flings as you want to with every fucking girl you meet. I am out. I never want to see you again. JUST GO AWAY.'

Every fucking girl? Now that was just a preposterous exaggeration!

'I am sorry—' I could barely speak; I wanted to cry and shout and wish I could go back in time and make it all right.

She turned around, 'Sorry? You are *sorry*? *I* am sorry, Joy. I say that to myself every day, to have invested so much into someone like you. I am sorry to have loved you so much and I am sorry to have thought that probably you were different from the others. But you know what? I regret that our names will be on the same piece of paper for so many years to come. I really do. Best of luck, Joy. I hope this book works, too, and you get whatever you are out there to get. Please don't ever try to contact me. I am doing great without you!'

She drove off and left me standing there in a haze of dust and smoke. Her words were heavy and cruel. And they made me feel like shit; I wanted to curl up and die.

All the attention just got to me. I had always been on the sidelines before, ignored and forgotten, and the little attention I got, I couldn't handle it; I screwed up. I couldn't resist the temptation. I cheated on her.

When Manika came to know about it, she couldn't bear the sight of me. She was pissed for two months and she spewed fire every time I tried contacting her. She had all the reasons to be mad at me. Even I was mad at myself for letting such a beautiful thing slip away. It was all my doing. It was already too late when I realized what I had lost in the bargain, and once again, I found myself on the floor, crying my heart out.

***

He had changed the names again. The second book wasn't Life, the Second Serving, *but it was something equally corny as the first book's name.*

'You are an asshole, I hope you know that,' I said. 'Exactly how many girls did you sleep with?'

'C'mon. Now don't start with that. I am already very guilty about it and I don't want to revisit that time again. I really meant no harm. It just happened,' he said.

'Whatever,' I said. 'Anyway, so how did things get better between the two of you?'

'A few months after our break-up, her job took her to Bangalore, though she kept coming back to Delhi once in a while. She had started dating someone,' he said, in not the happiest of tones.

'What? *Really?*'

'Yes. She did,' he said.

'So? What did you say?'

'What could I have? I felt a little bad. But then, I had let her down. I couldn't have said anything to her.'

'So, you were uncomfortable?'

'Yes, it killed me, but I learned to live with it. We started talking again and things became better, and we became friends again. Slowly, we started sharing everything. I was a little pissed off, though.'

'Pissed off? Why were *you* pissed off?'

'*She hardly took any time getting over me! And all her friends loved her new guy! I hated the guy she was dating.*'

'*Obviously, Joy. But were you dating too?*'

'*Yes, I was trying to, though none of them really worked out for me. I tried really hard to find someone but I couldn't. I felt really worthless that I was no longer a priority in Manika's life. Her new guy was!*'

'*Asshole,*' I said. '*But you had no right to be angry at her! You dumped her! She had full rights to push you down the priority order.*'

'*Whatever. No matter how many flings or relationships I had after it, she was always the top priority,*' he said.

'*That's nonsense. Anyway, let's just change the topic. Ummm . . . when did you join the business school?*'

'*After I got caught at my office leaving office early, paying guards to mark my attendance, faking time inputs and missing deadlines, the usual,*' he said and smiled.

'*By the way, that's not really the usual, it really doesn't happen with everyone. How can you be so casual about everything?*' I said, a little shocked by his apathy.

'*Ahh, skip that,*' he said and continued '*Did I tell you that even Manika joined a business school?*'

'*She took the CAT, too?*'

'*Yes! It was almost a shock to me. She wanted to go to MICA or something to study advertising, but she ended up in a regular management college in Bangalore. Such a waste! I tried to tell her that it wasn't a wise choice, but her boyfriend had convinced her that it was the most sane career choice. I still don't know why she did it,*' he said.

'*Spare me the boring details,*' I said.

'*Okay. Fine,*' he said. '*So . . .*'

***

Moving On

The guy Manika had started to date was nothing special, but Manika had started harping about how *dependable* and how *caring* and how *mature* he was. I just thought these are the words used for a guy when he is *super boring*. The first time she had told this to me over GoogleTalk, it *hurt*. It hurt like shit. I couldn't imagine what I would have gone through had she cheated on me. I kicked these thoughts out of my mind and tried to make myself happy for her. And in any case, it was just a rebound, and she was so trying to fling it in my face.

But truly speaking, though I really missed her a lot, I loved meeting all these new people, who already liked me even before they had met me. It was an easy life, you see. I didn't have to please anyone any more.

Though I always knew that Manika was probably the girl of my dreams and I used to spend hours pining for her and cursing her boyfriend; I loved the other parts of my life too—I *loved* the attention. The second book opened to worse reviews than the first one, but a lot of people loved it. Around that time, I got through MDI, a top ranking business school in Gurgaon and suddenly, I was a student again; it was a great feeling.

Over the next few months, I met some incredibly charming women in the college and outside, a few of whom I ended up dating, but nothing worked out; deep down I knew where my heart belonged and I tried to overlook that. But those charming women, the numerous short relationships, and dates, and break-ups gave me the subject of my third book—*Life. Final Serving*—and I wrote it during the first year of my postgraduation.

A girl named Surbi was my muse, who had decided to dump me for another guy, and it pained me. Male ego, I tell you. It's a terrible thing. I was angry and distraught, even though I forgave the girl almost instantly because I never loved her, so it was kind of a relief. I didn't love her as much as I hated the guy she left me for.

~

'The response is phenomenal!' Soumitra exclaimed about the third book.

It was surprising because I thought I would suck without Manika. Still, I thought I would stop writing after the third one. Since Manika was no longer with me in the scheme of things, the entire process had lost its charm and it was no longer fun. I had realized I would never match up to what we were when we wrote together.

'I think the book is pretty shitty,' Manika said. She was in town for some work and Soumitra had called us together.

All the animosity between Manika and me had vanished. We had proven those people wrong, who said that exes couldn't be friends.

'Yeah, you would say that,' Soumitra said, 'But everyone thinks that this third book is actually all true, that you guys broke up and that's why he wrote this one as a solo book! It's *brilliant*. People have been asking when the next one is coming up.'

'Whenever he dates another girl. Which is OFTEN,' she mocked.

'Very funny,' I said. 'I don't think I will write another one.'

'Why?' Soumitra said.

'I don't know.'

'Never mind. Take some time off, you deserve it. I am sure you will come up with something.'

I seriously doubted that. With Manika finally out of the equation, I was sure I no longer wanted to write. We left our publisher's office and I took Manika out to a nearby restaurant to treat her on the success of the third and the final book of the series.

'Are you still crying over the girl who dumped you for another guy?' she said.

'Nope, not anymore,' I said.

'But you do know that you write bullshit, right?'

'That I know. But then again, I write what people like to read,' I defended myself. 'At least, I didn't abandon them. I gave them the third book and brought closure to the series.'

'That's capitalist bullshit,' she said. 'Anyway, coffee?'

'Capitalist bullshit? You're saying that? You wanted to be a writer, a journalist, and now you're doing management in finance and marketing. You have to be the most capitalistic person alive!'

'Writing lost its charm,' she mumbled and I couldn't say anything to that.

'So is the book really bad?'

'It stinks. It's like, *really* bad,' she said. 'Anyway, let's not talk about that. I have been wanting to ask you, how did it feel being cheated upon?'

'It's pretty bad, I didn't really enjoy it,' I chuckled.

'I know.'

'But, it was still better. I didn't love her, but the mere fact that she dumped me for someone else, it just sucked,' I said, and gulped my coffee.

'It does. One just keeps thinking as to where did he or she go wrong? Why did the other person stray?' She looked at me.

I looked at her blankly, and then I changed the topic. 'But I am happy for you. You and Ravi.'

'Hmm,' she said and breathed heavily. 'And how is your *other* girlfriend?'

'Other girlfriend?'

'Sidharth. Who else?'

'Oh, I didn't tell you. He is coming back for a month to India.'

'Oh, he is?'

'Yes. And he is after my life to take leave for a month from college. It's impossible, and he is giving me all kinds of crazy ideas to go on road trips and stuff!'

'He will get you into trouble again.'

'I am sure he will. But I am asking you again and this is probably the millionth time. Why don't you come for my sister's wedding? You know it will be fun. The three of us, together again?'

'I want to. But you know I wouldn't get leave. You know how my college is, they are really strict! Later, maybe?' she said.

'Whatever.'

We shared three coffee lattes that evening and it was the best coffee I had had in a long time. I didn't want to say goodbye that day but then she had to go and I had no idea how to stop her from going. She was just a friend now.

**

'*This was the time you almost got married, right?*' I asked.

'*Yes. Crazy times,*' Joy said. '*And it was all due to Sidharth. As usual, he got me into trouble . . .*'

'*How?*'

'*It was my sister's wedding and there was this girl everyone liked and since she was insanely rich and her parents liked me, Sidharth almost made me say yes to her.*'

I laughed. '*And this was also the time of the stripper incident! Wasn't it?*'

'*Oh, yes! Who can forget that?*' he said, his eyes lighting up. '*Who knew what Sidharth would return with? I am sure his parents wouldn't have been proud had they known.*'

Joy went on with his narration.

**

Of Strippers and Love

'Joy,' Mom said, with seriousness writ all over her face. 'What do you plan to do?'

Frankly speaking, I was a little confused. My sister was getting married that week and I thought it was something related to that. But, pretty soon, I realized what the tone meant—she was talking about my *future*. Everyone around me was more interested in the wondrous possibilities of my future than me.

'Nothing. I mean, I haven't decided. Marketing, I guess. That's what my subject is in college,' I stuttered.

'You *guess*? One year from placements, shona, and you haven't decided? You had a perfectly fine job, I don't know why you decided to leave it and do management,' she said, her voice softening. 'You don't plan to write books as a career, do you?'

Obviously, I couldn't have told her that I was kicked out and scraping through to a half-decent management degree was my only option. Mom had always been mortally afraid of me taking up writing as a career. We are all brought up on images of poor writers, self-righteous engineers, upper-middle-class management graduates and scoundrel businessmen. She argued that being a writer is bad for the image of any guy. And although I had no plans to take up writing as full-time job, I often teased her, saying that it was exactly what I wanted to do. Dad always knew that I was kidding (or he knew I wasn't good enough).

'*Yes*, Mom. I plan to write for a living. That's what I have always wanted to do,' I said, and faked seriousness.

'So what? Let him write,' Dad said and chuckled. 'Let him do something different that no one else in the family has done.'

'Yes, it's good to have a writer in the household!' Di added, as she tried a piece of jewellery and rejected it.

'All of you are mad. And especially you . . .' Mom pointed at Dad. 'How will it be to say that our son sits home all day and writes? You can't call that a job! Chee, chee, chee.'

'I think it sounds cool,' Di said and looked at Dad. Dad smiled.

'Shona, why don't you do something like Sidharth? Look where he is!' Mom said.

'Sidharth is doing nothing,' Di said. 'Ask him when he comes tomorrow.'

Sidharth was to stay with us for my sister's wedding. Mom had always thought very highly of Sidharth, since he was always the engineer/researcher/academic type, the self-righteous type, and also because he ate a lot—Mom liked that.

'I will ask him. And I will also ask him to give you some common sense!' Mom said, and went to the kitchen, realizing that it was three against one. The rest of us looked at each other and smiled. My sister and my dad had confidence in me that I wouldn't totally screw up in life. And they had better things to do than worry about my career. Di had to get married in two days and Dad had to finish the Friday crossword.

'Hey,' Di called out. 'You saw that girl in pink in the function yesterday?'

'Who?' I asked.

'She is talking about Kanika. The groom's second cousin,' Dad said.

'Oh yes, what about it?'

'Joy, she is your age! And she is great-looking!' Di said.

'So?'

'So? Talk to her!'

'She is right,' Dad said and smiled again. He was doing a lot of smiling and laughing these days, quite opposite to what a bride's dad usually does. 'It will be easier for us to get the two of you married in the same family, gives us one less set of relatives to take care of!'

'Very funny,' I said.

'Arrey bhai, she is rich, too. Only daughter. And she is beautiful. I talked to her. She has even read your books. So *why* not?'

'Getting married into money? Seems like I have given the right education to my kids,' Dad said, and closed the newspaper. 'Let me tell your mom that her son is so poor that he wants to marry the only daughter of a rich man,' he chuckled and left the room. Luckily, the topic was never raised again, except once, when Sidharth totally brainwashed me into saying yes. Luckily, I didn't.

~

It had been three hours since I had been waiting at the airport, which was teeming with men and women and children in all sizes, waiting, some holding placards with names scrawled on them, and there was no sign of him anywhere around. I had started to get pissed off. I had already downed three big burgers and killed time at the bookshop nearby, buying books I knew I would never read. I really had nothing to do. I fixed my gaze on the Arrivals passage and sat on the ground. Another half an hour passed by before I saw him, and I was positively shocked!

He had not come alone. He had decided to bring along a souvenir with himself. *A big, fair one*—one that everyone at the airport was staring at.

What the fuck!?

I swore aloud as I saw him walk towards me. And it wasn't just I who did that. He kissed her. She almost had to bend to reach his lips. She had blonde hair, deathly white skin, and she was so tall it seemed her legs just started where I ended. As if Sidharth was not tall enough, this girl was even taller by a few inches. She was an electric pole and had the most perfect figure I could ever imagine on a girl that tall.

'Hey!' he shrieked aloud as he hugged me tight.

'Hey . . . how . . .' I said as he choked me.

'This is Liss.'

'Liss?' I said, as she came forward and hugged me and I felt her breasts brush against my face. It was awkward.

'Heard a lot about you,' she said in a strange accent, I guessed East European.

'Hmm . . .'

That's all I could say then. We took a taxi from the prepaid stand and we shifted our conversation to Hindi after I calmed down my nerves. My hands were sweaty and clammy.

'Who's she?'

'Liss. Just told you,' Sidharth said casually.

'I know her name, chuutiye. Who the fuck is she? And what the fuck is she doing with you? And will she fucking stay with us?'

He laughed out loud. The asshole was having some fun at my expense and curiosity.

'She is with me,' he said. 'And if you want, we can stay out somewhere. Just drop us to any guesthouse nearby and we will manage.'

Now what does one say to that? He knew I wouldn't let that happen. He had to stay with us because my mother would hear of nothing else. I stayed shut and imagined how horrified Mom would be to see the tall girl from Europe.

'You mean you are dating her?' I asked him, just to be sure.

'Yes,' he said, still smiling at me.

'Like really dating her? Like going out on dates, saying things to each other, that sort of stuff?' I asked, just to be more sure.

'Joy! I know what dating is, man!'

'Are you shitting me? Why in the world would she date you? And why the heck is she in India?'

'Could it be because of my sheer awesomeness? And that she loves me for it!' he said and shrugged his shoulders.

'Stop the fucking smiling, man, it's creepy. What's the story?'

After playing around with me a little longer, he told me—and I wasn't sure if I should believe his story. Liss was a stripper he came across in Poland; she used to dance in a joint named 'Spicy Peppers'. He went to her show seven days a week, all days in a month, and bought her drinks every single day. He was undeniably in love with her, and then one day, when a man twice Sidharth's size tried acting fresh with Liss, our guy went up onto the stage, took that man down and ended up with two hairline fractures and fifteen stitches. And as they say—the rest is history.

Sidharth was going out with a *stripper* and apparently, they were very much in love. I always thought strippers fell in love with very rich and very old men. Sidharth was neither! I had a hard time convincing myself that all of this was true and I was not watching a movie.

'And she still does those shows?' I asked.

'Yes dude. It's all business. I approve of it. She comes from a poor family and this is how she pays for her education. She is a double major. That's all I know. It's just been three weeks that we have been together! And it's been blissful!'

'Three weeks and you get her to my sister's wedding?' I said.

'Hey. You took one look to fall in love with Manika. Three weeks is a *long* time! Chill, Joy. And you know your mom loves me. She wouldn't mind,' Sidharth said.

Obviously she would! She is a tall white woman in a short skirt! At her daughter's wedding!

'Are you talking about me?' Liss butted in and smiled at us.

'Yes dear,' he said, and kissed her.

'You love her?' I asked him.

'I guess so.'

'Bullshit. And weren't you supposed to be in Paris? What the heck were you doing in Poland?'

'Cheap strip clubs, man. Cheap strip clubs. You should come there once . . . if there is heaven, it's there. It's there. It's there. I got a part of heaven for myself. Can you deny?' he said.

'So much for making your parents proud, Sidharth. They would be really happy to see this.'

~

There was silence. We all sat in the drawing room, Liss silently stared at everyone, I looked at Dad who tried hard not to smile and my sister and Sidharth had a whole conversation in looks and smiles and gestures. Though, what took the cake was the way Mom looked at Liss who kept crossing and uncrossing her legs (not a very smart move, that). It seemed like a giant wheel turning. It was hilarious!

'Hey. Why don't you kids go inside and talk?' Dad finally said, bowing down to Mom's look which said out aloud, *we-need-to-talk*!

'Fine,' I said, and we all rushed to the bedroom like freed animals from the zoo.

As we entered my bedroom, I could hear faint noises of Mom freaking out in Bengali outside while Dad was still laughing aloud. After a few minutes, Mom shut up as she always did, since Dad never gave up smiling and Mom conceded that there must be something amusing in the whole situation.

'So,' Di said. 'She seems to be calm now.'

Sidharth smiled.

'Girlfriend?' Di asked Liss.

'That's what he says,' Liss said.

'Where are you from?'

'She is from Hungary. But stays in Poland now,' Sidharth said.

'Did I ask you? And no wonder that accent. Very East European, very cool,' Di said. 'Student? Or working?'

'Both actually.'

'Oh, that's nice. I used to dream about paying for my own education by taking up a summer job or something, but it never materialized. I am almost jealous,' Di said.

'No, you are not. I am a stripper,' she said almost casually.

. . . and there was silence.

'Ummm,' Di said. 'I think you are too beautiful to be a stripper!'

'That's so sweet of you,' Liss said and blushed.

Had it been anyone else, he or she would have made a mess of the situation, but my Di has always been quite the wordsmith.

'Sidharth?' Di said. 'I am going to steal her away for a couple of hours. I am going shopping, because if she turns out in this mini skirt tomorrow, there will be more eyes on her than me and that's every bride's worst nightmare!'

Sidharth chuckled and Di continued, 'Let me get you some really ugly Indian clothes so that you don't look as pretty as you are.'

'I am sure you will look beautiful!' Liss said and hugged her. 'Sidharth made me watch a few Hindi movies. Indian brides look beautiful, it's much better than our boring white and black themes.'

Soon after, Di took Liss to her room and they left after a while. Sidharth was happy to see Di taking interest in showing Liss around; he heaved a sigh of relief.

'Nice,' Sidharth said. 'This is going better than I had imagined. See, I told you everything will be alright! Your sister loves her, and I think even your mom loves her!'

'Yeah, why not? I think she almost passed out,' I retorted.

'Chill, Joy, your mom loves me. I am not a broke writer like her son. I am a fucking engineering postgraduate student in Europe.'

~

'So, how does she look?' Di said as she turned Liss around. They had been gone for quite some time now. Sidharth and I meanwhile were wrapping up wedding errands Dad had put us on. He had a great time flirting with all my cousins while I was left to converse with sweetshop owners, tent fixers, and what not, all of whom were hell-bent on robbing me.

'I didn't know they made suits in her size!' I said. I had never seen a six-foot-two white girl wearing an Indian suit. Generally, I hate attempts of white women wearing Indian clothes and going in search of the truth, but Liss looked splendid.

'She . . . she looks . . . fabulous!' Sidharth said with his eyes wide open and his mouth agape.

'Do I?' Liss said.

'Yes, you do,' Sidharth said and they kissed. 'You always do. You always will.'

'Okay then, I will leave the three of you,' Di said. 'Joy, Mom, Dad and I are going to someone's place, Dinner is on the table, so you can eat and sleep. We will be late.'

I nodded. Liss and Di hugged and she left.

'How do you like it?' I asked Liss.

'It's very nice. In Hungary or even in Poland, we don't wear things with such bright colours and embellishments,' she said, looking at her green and blue suit with Swarovski crystals stitched all over it. 'I hope I will not feel overdressed.'

'It's an Indian wedding, svizi!' Sidharth said. 'If anything, you will feel underdressed.'

I Googled 'svizi' later and it came out to be the Hungarian word for cutie; the terms of endearments sound a lot cornier when other people use them, not otherwise. I wasn't trying not to see this, but now I had begun to believe Sidharth was in *love* with this girl. They were both into each other, their body language reminiscent of how Manika and I used to be, the holding of hands, the frequent kissing and the lingering stares weren't just raging hormones. Even in a room filled with other people, they were constantly stealing glances at each other and smiling; it was ridiculously cute and it made me feel sad and lonely.

Sidharth and Liss slept on my bed that day, and I slept on a mattress on the ground, wallowing in self-pity and self-hate. Just as I was drifting off to sleep, I heard a few utensils crash outside. I thought it was Di and went outside to check if everything was all right. It was her last night in the house and I thought it was natural not to get enough sleep. I went outside to check up on her, and saw Di and Liss talking and laughing.

'Hi, Joy,' Di said.

'Not sleepy?' I asked her.

'I am now,' she said. 'I will hit the bed. There is some warm milk in the saucepan if you want. Good night!'

'Goodnight,' Liss and I echoed.

She smiled and went off to sleep. Even Di was lucky. She never fell in love before, never even had a relationship, and fell for the guy my parents chose for her. Within days of their first official meeting, the one where both sets of parents were present, they were lying to their parents and sneaking out, and watching movies, going out on dates and holding hands.

Everybody had triple Aces or a full house and I was still with a Joker in hand.

'Not sleepy?' I asked Liss.

'No,' she said and sipped her milk. 'You have got a wonderful family. My parents got divorced when I was six. I have not seen my dad since.'

'I am so sorry.'

'Don't be. I never saw much of him even before. And he used to abuse me. So it's all right. I really don't care now. You have to know the person to hate him or her.'

'Mom?' I asked.

'She died a few years back. Alcohol problem,' she said, as her eyes welled up and she blinked them away.

'Everything will be fine,' I said. 'And hey! You have Sidharth now. He is a great guy!'

'I know. He's too good to be with me, maybe. He has everything, he doesn't need me. Annyira aranyos, szeretem őt annyira,' she said and looked away.

'I really didn't get the last part because I don't speak Hungarian, but I wish I did because then I would have a shot at someone who's so sweet and charming and pretty! I am happy for him and I know he loves you,' I said.

'You really think he loves me?' Liss asked, with unsure eyes and quivering lips.

'You think he will get a girl from Poland to meet me and my family unless he really loves her? He looks stupid, but he really isn't.'

'I don't know.'

'Anyway, a fun fact, did he tell you what happened to the guy his ex-girlfriend cheated-dated with?' I said, trying hard to change the mood.

'What? No! Tell me,' she said.

'He got him beaten and bashed. I still can't forget that day. It was blood and guts all over, and he even trashed his car. He's quite a badass.'

'Really?'

'Yes. With Sidharth, it's always the whole distance. No half measures. I am sure that guy never saw a worse day,' I said.

'But this time around, he was the one who got beaten, pretty badly! I was surprised when from nowhere he lunged at the guy and started punching him. It was so cute because he's so small and the guy was HUGE,' she said and chuckled.

'Sidharth is NOT small!'

She chuckled and said, 'Small by our standards! Hey. Can I ask you for a favour? You have to promise me you won't tell him.'

'I won't.'

'Can you ask him about what he feels about . . . umm . . . my *job*?' she said, teary-eyed. 'Don't tell him I asked you to.'

'Ummm,' I said. 'I asked him that the moment I met you. He will never stop you from doing it; neither will he show any signs of dissent. But I can tell you that it probably kills him to see you do what you do in front of unknown men. He would do anything to make you not do what you do. But I don't think he will ever tell you that.'

'Thank you,' she murmured. 'Okay, enough about me. What about you? No girlfriends? Nothing? Sidharth told me that you are a bit of a celebrity around here.'

'Naah! You should know how he exaggerates. I am single. I guess I never found the right girl. Maybe you should set me up with one of your stripper friends.'

'You will have to come to Poland for that,' she said and chuckled. We sipped on our milk. She continued, 'I don't know much, but Sidharth says you really love the girl you wrote your first book with, Manika?. Did I get the name right?' Liss said.

'Spot on. I guess I did, but that's all in the past. She has a boyfriend now and she is pretty happy with him. He is a nice guy and all her friends really like him.'

I must have looked away, or my face probably fell, because she didn't ask me anything further. We talked about her time in Hungary and Poland, and what she wanted to do, and what she wanted to study, and then we warmed up another saucepan of milk and chatted a while before we felt sleepy and went to bed. I slept that night, thinking of Manika and wishing she was there for my sister's wedding. I thought of calling her but then changed my mind. It would have been good had she been there. But as we had always said to each other—*it wasn't meant to be.*

***

'So, what next?' I said. 'You went back to Manika or what?'

'I tried,' Joy said and winked. 'I called. I wanted to tell her that I loved her. But I thought it was a stupid idea. She was already in a serious relationship and it didn't make sense to pull her out from something real and promise her something I myself was not sure I could deliver. So I just called and told her that I wished she could be at the wedding.'

'Lame,' I said. 'I remember the wedding, though! Di looked amazing! I remember Liss too. Sidharth and she were constantly at their public displays of affection. You were pretty angry at them, weren't you? So was your mom, I think, I remember you complaining. They left early, didn't they?'

'You remember quite a lot, don't you! Sidharth was happy that day. Liss had just told him that she would quit her job and take up something at the supermarket. And the next day, they were off on an all-India tour. He tried to tag me along, but I couldn't go. If only I had gone with them, you wouldn't have put me in trouble! You made my life miserable!'

'Your life was already miserable. All you did was think of Manika, be a little bitch and cry! I just wanted to set you up with a friend. It's not my fault that she was a complete bitch,' I said.

'*Whatever. So anyway, there was this friend of mine, Neeti,*' he said. And I smiled.

'*Neeti?*' I asked.

'*Why?*' Joy said. '*You want me to change your name too?*'

***

The Disappointment

'Get out of here! You have been single for six months? I thought you were *famous*! Seems like you're not. You found no one?' she asked.

'Let's just say that I am still looking for the right girl.'

'You don't look the kind who looks for the right girl,' Neeti said. 'You're the one who makes mistakes, a lot of them.'

Neeti had been a back-burner friend since long. Though I had known her for the last six years or so, I had never really met her that often. Either I was busy being a doting boyfriend, or I was in the dumps, crying, wailing.

Except for Manika, she was probably the only girl that I had really felt some connection with. But of late, Neeti and I had started spending some time together and it was fun to share things with her. She was never judgemental about the choices I made and had a sympathetic ear.

That day, we were at her place celebrating her birthday, and I was co-hosting and even though I was in-charge of drinks and the cake and the lights, I had done nothing. I had just agreed because she had promised it was an all-girls party and I could look at some pretty women and be less depressed about losing Manika to my stupidity.

'You are just trying too hard to find your true love, to try and replace Manika,' Neeti shouted behind all the noise. It was horrible music, I should have been in charge of that.

'I am trying too hard? I am not even trying. I am just sitting here wondering if one of your friends would slowly shed their skin, like a snake, and turn into Manika. Other than that, I am just clocking time until we perfect the science behind cloning.'

'Don't worry. You will find someone,' she said. 'It's hard to find someone who would like things that you do. No one wants to sit at home with a guy and read books.'

'You mean to say that girls these days would rather put make-up on than be intelligent and thoughtful?'

'You get it,' she said and laughed.

'Chill, Neeti! I will forever be alone and I am resigned to that fate,' I said. She made a nasty face. 'That's not too bad. I don't write books any more but at least I can act and live like an author, poor and lonely!'

'Okay. Then what about her?' she pointed to a girl in a short black dress, already a little tipsy and shouting at the top of her voice.

'Too slutty,' I shouted.

'What about her? She is a doctor, not clingy and very smart. I am sure she even likes books and shit,' Neeti suggested.

'If she is so freaking smart, I am sure she will not fall for me,' I screamed into her ear.

'*Why?* You are an author for heaven's sake. Anyway, find one on your own. I will go mix around, or people will think we are an item. And I certainly don't want to get counted in the list of bimbos you have been out with.'

'Funny,' I said.

She left me there and walked into a crowd of drunk, happy people. I didn't know many people there so I shifted my attention to the appetizers and the beer. Slowly and steadily, I was about five beers down, mostly because I was insanely bored, and my head had started to spin. I found a place to sit. My courage levels had gone up since I was a little drunk, so I sat near a very pretty girl. She wasn't so much as pretty as she was sexy. Dark skin, long legs, and she wore a *very* short and intriguing skirt! She sat there alone, sipping on a cocktail, I don't know which, through the most incredibly red luscious lips; she looked exotic.

'Hi,' I said, after a few seconds passed.

She smiled back and looked away.

'How do you know Neeti?' I asked again after a while.

'Through common friends. I don't really know her personally.'

'I am Joy,' I said, and thrust out my hand.

'I know,' she said and shook my hand.

'You know?'

'The guy who writes love stories and romances, my friends read your books, and I don't think they like them very much,' she said dispassionately.

The conversation was just not going anywhere and my numerous attempts at keeping it alive just fell flat. It was a lost cause. Bored and defeated, I got up and went outside for some fresh air. I didn't know how long I stood there with my eyes closed, but when I opened them, she was there again, in the corner, smoking. She faintly reminded me of Manika. I watched her from the corner of my eye as she stubbed out the cigarette and tried lighting another one. The lighter spewed sparks, but no flame. She tried and tried again.

'Got a light?' she gestured.

'I don't smoke.'

'You don't smoke? I didn't think authors were non-smokers. Maybe *real* authors are non-smokers.'

'Real authors? Is that even a term?' I retorted.

'C'mon. You know what kind of books you write. They are repetitive and the grammar is poor and the language is pedestrian. I don't know why publishers even publish such books.'

'There is a separate market for every product and don't judge me when I say that books are products. But you can draw a successful analogy. Just like your cigarette. You like it, so people are there to make it. It is poison, but what the heck!'

She looked away and said, 'So you do know that what you write is poison.'

'I don't. That's not what I meant. See, you're misquoting me.'

'A guy who writes but doesn't have the right words to say what he really means. Now that tells a lot about how you write,' she smiled disdainfully.

'Fine. Whatever. I don't write anymore. I'm a management student so you can be happy about that,' I said. She was pissing me off now.

'You should stick to to that,' she hissed.

'What do you have against the kind of books I write?'

'They are all bullshit love stories, which follow the same trajectory. The guy falls in love, it's all good, then everything goes down and then a happy ending. You show the youth as a bunch of confused, clueless people,' she grumbled.

'You hate my books and still you read them and then you say you're not confused,' I smirked.

'I have just read three of your books,' she defended, her icy-cold stare piercing through me.

'I have written just three,' I mocked.

'I read them just to see if you had improved,' she said, unconvincingly.

'And I don't think you have a problem with what I write. I think you have a problem with every book ending on a good note, that your own life is not a fairytale and is probably in a mess,' I laughed; maybe I shouldn't have.

'So now you are a psychiatrist?' she scoffed. 'Anyway, I need to go,' she turned around and opened the balcony gate.

'Umm . . . I didn't get your name.'

'Natasha,' she said and disappeared into the crowd.

Nice girl, I said to myself. I hadn't been around a lot of them lately. Plus, I figured it wouldn't be too bad to be back in a nice, stable relationship.

***

'*I know how the story went from there on,' I said. 'You know what, Joy. You have always made your life tougher for yourself. It has always been your fault.*'

'*I know that. Don't make me feel bad about it,' Joy said. 'But it was horrible, right? Remember?*'

'*Yes. You drove me up the wall just to get her number. And then Natasha broke your heart. Made you wait for three weeks for the first date. Another month for the second date and after three months of making out with you, you got to know that she was already dating someone for the past three years.*'

'*You had really started keeping track of me, hadn't you?*'

'*I had to! You were so darn suicidal in those days. And you told me the story about a million times. You were depressed and it was terrible. Believe me.*'

'*I know it was terrible, but we spent three months together, and to realize that it was all a big lie was shattering. Her absence wasn't as damaging as the loss of my belief in dating and love and relationships, and you know how strongly I believe in love. I was distraught; it was as if what I did with Manika was coming back to me. It was a dark and a horrible time.*'

'*Thank God for Sidharth and Liss. And Manika, of course.*'

'*Yep,' Joy said, embarrassed.*

190

It was a devastating time for Joy. All of us really thought Joy was kidding at first, because it wasn't the first time his relationship had failed and he was in inconsolable sobs, but he stopped going to college and his grades dipped. It was really bad. He used to call me and cry like a little girl for hours. Although he really doesn't talk about it all that much, we all remember it. Sidharth. Liss. Manika. None of us could talk him out of his depression. We all hated that bitch, Natasha.

The shock of Natasha being with someone else while she was with him was too much for him to take. Natasha had always treated Joy like shit, and maybe her disinterest in him was the reason for his unending interest in her. And though Natasha was pretty hot, she had to be, she was a struggling model for quite some time, she really didn't deserve all the money and the time Joy showered on her. He had convinced himself that she was the one; he was really desperate.

When the relationship ended, everything fell apart like a pack of cards. I remember the post-break-up days when he used to stay locked up for weeks at a stretch and not move out of his house; it had been a few months since his parents had moved out and shifted to a different city and he was left to fend for himself, at which he did a very poor job. We were really worried about him.

Sidharth was somewhere in Kerala, backpacking with Liss, when all this happened and he was pissed at how much of a cry baby Joy was. He just said Joy would cry and wail and want to die and then eventually get over it, something that I didn't see happening.

Sidharth conjectured that Joy wanted to be with Natasha only because he didn't want to be alone while Manika was still dating somebody. He needed somebody, he needed to be in a relationship, and feel loved. Sidharth believed Joy was still in love with Manika. And that is why he was cribbing about the whole Natasha thing. 'He's such a pussy' were his exact words for Joy.

Manika understood it better. And though we managed to keep his outbursts in check, it was really hard to get him to behave normally. His behaviour was getting worse each passing day, he wouldn't eat, he wouldn't bathe or shave, and he refused to talk to anybody. I remember having a chat with Manika just before she was coming to Delhi for her internship.

'I am thinking of moving in with him if he allows me to,' she said. 'Just temporarily. Have you seen how much weight he has lost? Such a wrong time for his parents to shift out of Delhi.'

'It will be great if you can be with him,' I said. 'Is your internship in Delhi throughout?'

'Yes. I will be coming to Delhi next week, and my internship will start from the week after that. At least it's good that he, too, is doing his internship in Delhi. Though, I wonder if he will even turn up at his workplace, seeing his present state of affairs,' Manika said.

'If anyone can make a difference, it's you. You know him best.'

'I am not sure if I know him at all. It's so strange seeing him like this,' she said. 'I have never seen him act so strangely before.'

'But won't your boyfriend mind? Ravi—if I remember correctly, right?' I asked and she said she would handle it.

Joy turned down the idea of Manika staying with him and told her that he didn't need anyone's help or sympathy, and Manika told him she had rented a flat near Joy's residence. But very often, she would stay over for a couple of days at his place. Slowly, she started living there, like Joy used to stay with her back in his engineering days. Manika was really concerned about Joy. I really felt Joy deserved what he got for what he did to Manika. He really didn't deserve a cute person like Manika.

'Things got better when she moved in, didn't they?' I said.

'They sure did,' Joy smiled and went on with his narration.

***

A Healing Heart

Manika was a breath of fresh air. I was glad her internship brought her to Delhi and she was staying with me. Ravi didn't know about it and she had planned to keep it that way. She took real good care of me. She had always been a great cook and I had always been a big fan of her culinary talents!

Anyway, slowly and steadily, I think it was her cooking that pulled me out of the depression. Whatever she did, it was working. The crying in the nights had stopped. The not-eating sessions and then the binge eating sessions had stopped, too. I was sleeping more on my bed rather than the couch and I didn't wake up with wet pillows beneath my head. Manika made me delete all pictures of Natasha from the laptop. She even found the hidden folders and deleted them. She blocked Natasha's Facebook profile and deleted the other profile I had made just to keep track of her. Things were beginning to get to normal within the first or second week itself. I was starting to get over Natasha.

A couple of days before the first day of our internship, we were out shopping for our formal clothes for our internships and she bought herself a few shirts in different shades of blue and pink and white, all of which fit her snugly, and a few pairs of pencil-fit trousers that matched the shirts; she looked very investment-banker-like. We kept it simple while buying for me: a few white shirts and a few dark blue trousers and two pairs of shoes.

Once we thought we had bought enough to last the length of our internships, we trundled to an eating joint nearby. She ordered white sauce pasta and I ordered noodles and some chicken.

'Joy?' Manika said. 'You know what, it's almost insulting how depressed you are after losing her, since you never really had her in the first place.'

'Why is it insulting?'

'You didn't shed a single tear when we parted!' she said and slurped a long winding string of pasta. 'In fact I guess you were pretty happy about it. And now that you have broken up with Natasha, look at you! You're a mess.'

'So what? You were nothing different! You can't blame me for something you did too. You went ahead and made a boyfriend within a few months of breaking up with me! That, too, a pretty serious one,' I said.

'Joy, I was devastated. I needed someone to pull me out of the mess, and he was there, guiding me, consoling me, because you were too busy with your little dates.'

'Actually, when we broke up, I never thought we would stay away from each other for long. I thought you would eventually miss the awesome sex and come running to me!' I chuckled. She didn't find it funny.

'Shut up,' she said. 'You lost your chance, Joy. You dropped the ball. Stop hitting on me now!'

'I know I did,' I said. 'How's the pasta? These noodles suck, so oily.'

'It's equally bad. I don't know why you wanted to come to this shitty place, as if the food isn't bad enough, their service sucks, too. We could have gone someplace nice. You're such a miser.'

'At least I got you here. My Plan A was to go back home, make you cook, read a book, and then go to sleep.'

'Stop spreading your depression around, Joy! For heaven's sake! Okay, I know an Italian place where we can go. Awesome food and it's pretty cheap, too. Plus they have very generous happy hours, if you want to drink!' she said, pushing her plate of generously slimy pasta away from her.

She left me no choice; we paid the bill for the food we hadn't eaten and after about an hour and a half, we reached the nice Italian place she was talking about earlier. The restaurant was dimly lit with candles, the engravings on plates and forks and the knives were complex and beautiful, a huge chandelier hung down from the high ceiling, and the waiters were nattily dressed.

'This seems expensive,' I whispered in Manika's ear. 'We are so out of place here.'

'You would be out of place. I am born for this,' she said, winked, and the manager whipped out a table near the artificial fountain.

'I feel so awkward with all these rich people around,' I said.

'But you're a fucking writer, Joy. You should be at ease anywhere you go. You're allowed to be awkward and out of place and goofy,' she said.

'Correction. A bad author,' I said.

'Well, that's true, but at least you're well read. That's got to count for something, right?' she said.

'Yeah, it makes me a nerd,' I answered. She asked me to shut up and we ordered roasted lamb chops, fettuccine Campania and a couple of Long Island Iced Teas to wash down our food with; despite cursing the noodles at the roadside restaurant I had eaten a lot and I was considerably full.

'So, tell me about Natasha,' Manika said, her chin resting on her knuckles.

'Tell you what?'

'Anything. What do you like about her? Anything special? What reminds you of her? What do you think when you think of her?'

'I don't want to talk about her,' I protested.

'No, please do. Let's get it out of your system. Go. Start talking or I will punch this fork right through your heart. Tell me anything about her,' she said and waved the fork around.

'Okay, okay . . .'

'Go on,' she said. 'Anything!'

'Natasha? She has three strands of grey hair that she absolutely hates; she has two tiny moles on the left foot; she likes her coffee without sugar in the mornings, and with two spoons full of it in the evening; she always puts the left shoe first before the right; she always carries ballerina shoes with her just in case; she hates to sleep with a pillow, prefers bolsters instead; and she uses a kiwi flavoured lip balm because everyone else uses a strawberry flavoured one.'

'Okay. That's an impressive start. You remember quite a lot, don't you?' Manika said and stuffed her mouth with a piece of bread, not impressed at all.

'Thank you,' I said. 'But I was just kidding. I made that all up. If I think of it now, I think I hardly knew her. Thank you for asking that question.'

'Thank you? *Why?*'

'I couldn't think of anything about her. I guess at certain levels, Sidharth was right. Maybe I am just used to being in a relationship.'

'Hey!' She shrieked and I figured she wasn't even listening to me.

'What? What?' I said.

'Look!'

'What? Where?' I looked at the direction of her hand.

'Isn't that her? Your girlfriend from school? The one with the long legs!'

'Sarah!' I gasped.

'*Go!* Say hi!' she said. 'She was after all your first kiss! Go meet her.'

'I am not doing that!'

'Why? Why not? You always thought she was pretty hot . . . go!'

'We parted on bad terms and I have never seen her since. I am not going up there. It will be quite strange.'

'C'mon! It's been five years now!' she said. 'Go on!'

'Okay. Maybe I should,' I said and got up from our table, and as I walked towards her, she looked at me. She recognized me and both of us broke out into smiles. Seeing her smile, the guy who was with her with his back towards us, turned in my direction and our eyes met.

It was Arnab! Arnab? I thought of turning around, but it was too late. She had seen me now, and so had Arnab. I hate coincidences.

'Hey,' I said as the two of them stood before me. It was *awkward*.

'Hi, Joy,' she said. 'Long time.'

'Yes. Very long. Hi, Arnab.' We shook hands. Arnab was still as fat and bald as I remembered from the last time I had seen him on Facebook. Even Sarah had gained considerable weight and her cheeks were puffy. They looked like siblings.

'You look great,' I said. Well, lied.

'Thank you,' Sarah replied. 'You look good, too.'

'So, you two? Like, you are together?' I asked.

'Yes, we are,' Arnab said. 'Why don't you join us? And we will tell you . . .'

It was strange—the animosity, the hatred, and the bad blood between Arnab and me had evaporated in an instant.

'I would have loved to but I am with someone here.'

'So what? Ask her to join in too,' Sarah said.

I protested vehemently because it was still awkward but soon the four of us were sitting together at their table, exchanging smiles and numbers, and passing food to each other and narrating anecdotes.

'So, Manika, you guys are still dating? I saw the last book didn't have your name on it,' Arnab asked Manika.

'No. We used to. Not anymore. You used to read our books? I am surprised.'

'Naah. But I do see the updates on your profile,' he said and chuckled.

'But how come you guys are together again? Joy told me that you guys broke up, then Joy started dating Sarah, and there was a huge fight between the three of you and all of you swore not to talk to each other again?' Manika asked and I looked at them, embarrassed and listless.

Arnab smiled and answered, 'After the huge fight that you just mentioned, I realized what an ass I had been, letting her go. I should never have. I mean, within a few days, I was miserable and lonely.'

'What did you do?' Manika asked.

'I went out and got her back! It was tough, and she really made me wait before she finally buckled and gave in. And that is after *she* was the one who made out with my best friend back then! It was her fault really.'

'Shut up! I had the right to do so. You had dumped me for no reason at all! But he was pretty persuasive,' Sarah said. 'Three days, three nights, he spent outside my house, just to get me to talk to him. It was very sweet. He followed me around, bought me things and asked for my forgiveness at least a million times. You can't say no to that, can you?'

'Aww! That's sweet,' Manika said and looked lovingly at Arnab.

'And after that, everything was history. He has been the sweetest, clingiest boyfriend ever. Now the sweetest fiancé!' she said and flashed her ring, huge and sparkly.

'What? No way!' I let out.

All three of them looked at me strangely. It was awkward again.

'That's beautiful,' Manika said and broke the awkwardness. I still wasn't out of the shock.

'You guys are getting married? Unbelievable!' I said. 'Seems only yesterday when he was trying to get rid of you. But aren't you too young to get married?'

'It will be a crime to let a good thing go,' he smiled and kissed Sarah.

'Aw!' Manika said and clutched my hand. What's so *awww* in seeing two fat people kiss? Only Hollywood stars look good when they kiss!

~

'See, I told you it would be fun to go out. You met your old friends!' Manika said as we got back home.

I was still reeling under the shock that Arnab and Sarah were together again. And this time, it was forever (which is death really, but yeah, forever).

'It's unbelievable that they are getting married. And after what happened. It's crazy. How things change!' I said.

'Yes, look at you!' Manika retorted.

'But you shouldn't have told them about Natasha and the whole depression thing. It's embarrassing.'

'But you *are* depressed, aren't you?' she winked.

'I am not! Not anymore. See, I am happy, I am smiling,' I flashed my teeth.

'Are you?' she said and her phone beeped out loud. 'Okay, shut up, it's Ravi.' She picked up the call, went inside the room and bolted the door.

I sat outside, still going through what had happened that evening. Arnab and Sarah! It was crazy. They were getting married at the year-end. It made me feel stupid about myself. They were getting married and moving on with their lives and I was crying myself hoarse over a girl whom I had just met weeks before. I was still being juvenile and stupid. Somewhere deep inside, when we were sitting there with them in that stupid, expensive Italian restaurant eating the stupid pasta with Manika by my side, it felt so right. Manika and I, together, behaving like a couple, with a couple—it seemed so perfect, but she had a boyfriend, and she was talking to him on the phone, door locked and far from me.

I switched on the television and flipped through the channels. And suddenly, I heard muffled shouts from Manika's room. I turned down the volume and tried to listen. I crept up to her bedroom door, the one she had occupied in my flat, and pinned my ear on the door. I could hardly hear anything.

'What?' Manika said as she opened the door and found me leaning against the wall with my ear against the door.

'Oh, I am sorry,' I said, 'I just heard some noises. What happened?'

'Ravi knows.'

'What? What does he know?'

'He knows that I am living with you,' she said, wiping her tears on her sleeve.

'What? You didn't tell him? I thought he knew!'

'Are you stupid, Joy? Why would he allow me to live with another guy?' she said, still crying a little. 'And that too it's *you*.'

'So? *Why* did you? You shouldn't have lied to him!' I said.

'You needed me, Joy. I knew what I was doing. And I didn't know he would get to know,' she said.

'Now what? What did he say?'

'Nothing. I handled it. He will be okay with it,' she said.

'You are moving out tomorrow. Your flat is barely minutes away. I can come over to your place anytime, no issues. And moreover, Manika, I am fine now. I don't want to be the reason behind any trouble with you and Ravi. I have already made you go through a lot.'

'Shut up, Joy. I am not going anywhere. I came when I felt like it and I will go when I feel like it. And I said I handled it. He is okay with it now. I will leave when I want to! Stop pushing me out of your life like you always do,' she said, went inside the room and banged the door behind her.

'She fought with him because of you?'

'Yes.'

'So sweet of her,' I said.

'She had always been unrealistically sweet,' Joy said. 'It was in her nature. She couldn't help it.'

'Did she shift?'

'Nope. I tried convincing her for days, but she said things were fine between the two of them. She stayed on. I didn't want her to go, you know. I wanted her to stay with me.'

'And how was your depression thereafter?'

'It vanished. It was like Natasha never existed!' he said. 'Things were back to where they were. I got over that stupid phase. I was back in the Manika phase of life!' he smiled. 'And the Manika phase of life had always been awesome.'

'You are such an asshole. So what happened after that?'

'I met Nisha again,' Joy said.

'That eight-year-long crush of yours? You are kidding me!'

'I am not!' he said.

Joy continued his narration.

***

202

The School Reunion

'You are back early!' Manika said as I entered through the main door. A month had passed since she had moved in and life couldn't have been better. We had surrounded ourselves with books and good food and sitcoms again.

Sidharth and Liss had moved in with us after their India tour that had stretched out to three months. Sidharth had taken a semester off from Paris and so had Liss, so both of them had a full six months to themselves. They were turning out to be quite a couple. They were *fun*! We partied, ate out, shopped, and got drunk like crazy! *Every day!*

Meanwhile, Manika and Ravi kept fighting but they always patched up after a few days. After one such fight, Manika started making plans to shift to her own place, but Sidharth and Liss asked her to stay on, and she did. I stayed shut but I was happy when she decided that she would stay on for the month. Thank God for Sidharth and his persuasive abilities.

'Where are the other two?' I asked.

'They told me they had to attend a party; free drinks for expatriates. They are lucky, they don't have to work!' she said.

'Yeah. Sure they are,' I said. 'But anyway, why are we being so sad? Our internship gets over in about a month and we will be back to being college students. You will have to go back to Bangalore and that sucks though.'

'Yes, it does. Oh, by the way, Sarah called. She said you didn't call her back.'

'Oh, I forgot!' I said. 'What did she have to say?'

'She was saying something about the school reunion this Saturday. She was asking if we could come. She said you told her that you would let her know but you never called her back. Are you avoiding her?' Manika asked.

'I am not in the mood. Plus, these reunions are really boring. Initially, it is when you see all these familiar faces, and then you realize you have nothing to talk to and it becomes boring and awkward,' I grumbled. 'I really don't want to go. I am not attached to my school at all.'

'They actually wanted to go out and have dinner with us after that,' she said, yearningly. I had killed her spirit so much, that she almost whispered the sentence. I wished I could kiss her and tell her how cute she was.

And yes, about kissing her. I don't know *how* I had been holding out. I wanted to kiss and hug Manika a zillion times every day, even though she never really wore the satin nightdresses anymore. The time when she cooked, watched television, washed clothes, read books to me, did her Pilates, hung out the clothes to dry—you get the drift, every time I was near her, I wanted to snuggle the life out of her. But I couldn't. She was someone else's. And it had started to bother me.

'As long as we leave early from school, I am fine. I will call up Arnab and tell him that we are coming.'

'Sure,' she said and smiled.

~

'Fucking asshole! You are not coming?' I barked at Arnab as he cancelled on me. 'You know this could be the reason for us not talking for the next five years, too. Fuck you, man.'

He said something about a flat tyre and no mechanic for miles, said he was very sorry and hung up. I felt like shit, as I drove into the parking lot of my school. I just didn't want to go back to that place.

'Oh. Nice building,' Manika said. 'They are not coming, are they?'

'Nope. Should we just go?' I asked. 'It's going to be really boring inside.'

'At least show me your classes and stuff, Joy. Then we will go. I promise,' she squeezed my hand.

'There is nothing to see! And you know how much I hated my school!' I protested.

As I said that, someone from my old class spotted me and waved at me. NOW, I was stuck.

'Hey, Joy! Long time! And you have changed,' the guy from my old high school class said.

'So have you,' I said, trying hard to recall his name.

'Great to see you, Joy. I will rush inside. See you in a while, right?'

'Right,' I said. We shook hands and he dashed inside.

'Who was he?' Manika said.

'I have no idea,' I said. 'Let's go inside.'

Inside, our juniors were performing some dance number, then a rock show, some speeches, a small skit, a funny one at that! And I have to admit, it wasn't boring. I remembered the time when we were kids . . . we were really an untalented bunch. These guys did a hell lot of things.

'They are good, aren't they?' I nudged Manika.

'I thought you hated your school and everything about it!'

'*What?* No! I never hated my school. I said I hated what *I* was in school! I was ugly and shy and detestable, and I think I am still those things,' I said, winked and got back to watching the play.

'Whatever,' she said.

And suddenly, I heard my name being called from the back. Once. Twice. Thrice. It was a familiar female voice, soft and gentle and haunting.

'*Joy!*'

'What?' I said and looked behind. 'What? *What?* Nisha?'

'Heeyyyy!' she said as she walked up to me and we hugged. I still don't know why we did that, but we did. Now, '*the hug*' was the maximum extent of my physical contact with the longest crush of my life. It had been preceded by Nisha and I shaking hands (a long, long time ago).

'You have changed!' Nisha said.

'And you are still the same! A little older perhaps. But yes, more or less!' I said. 'Still very cute!'

'Oh, so you can say that now? You had problems saying that in school! You used to be so shy, Joy!' she said and giggled.

'Very funny,' I said.

'And this must be Manika!' she said in her still chirpy voice.

'Hi,' Manika said and Nisha literally hugged the life out of her. Manika looked at me in sheer surprise.

'But how do you know?' I asked, very surprised.

'Hmmm, it's a small story. An interesting one, though,' Nisha said. 'See that guy?' she pointed to a guy laughing and frolicking around with a few girls I remembered from my class; they had all got older. They were Nisha's friends, I recalled. 'He is my boyfriend. And you know what the first thing he gifted me was?'

'Umm?' I said.

'Your book!' she exclaimed. 'And he said he wanted our relationship to be like Deboshree and Avik! That means, you two!'

'No kidding,' I said.

'I am not. And it was such a beautiful book! I have read all three. Many times over! They are all brilliant, though I like the first one the most. It is so touching and honest and refreshing!'

'You are being generous,' I said.

'Anyway, so that's how I know you,' she said and held Manika's hand. 'You guys are such an inspiration. The perfect couple! I wish I and Himanshu could be like you,' she giggled.

Manika smiled.

'Okay listen,' she said. 'I need to go now, but here is my card. Give me a call and we can all go out sometime? The four of us! It will be so much FUN!' she shrieked. 'And Manika, I can tell you about how he had a crush on me when we were little!'

'I would love to hear that,' Manika said and gave her a fake smile.

'Okay now. Ciao!' She said, handed over her business card, hugged us both and left.

Phew! Did this girl giggle a lot or what?

'Joy,' Manika said as soon as Nisha walked away, 'you had a crush on *her*?'

'Seems strange now. It's like she is yet to grow up,' I said.

'I can see that!' Manika said.

'But back then, I was nuts about her.'

'She is kinda adorable, though. But what's with the constant giggling? You *liked* that, Joy?'

'It seemed charming to me then. And you have to admit the giggling would have sounded endearing on a small girl, wouldn't it? But now, I would kill myself.'

'That's rude,' Manika said. 'She just said such good things about you!'

'Screw her,' I said.

She winked at me and clutched my hand. She whispered in my ear, 'Now that's called moving on!'

'Now that was strange!' I said.

'I know, ask me. The longest crush of my life turns out to be such a freak! Well, not a freak, but she was so insanely girlish and giggly. She was still the little girl I had had a crush on. Anyway, I was over her. But I have to give her some credit, she had my heart in her palms when I was kid. It still gives me the shivers thinking about how obsessed I was back then,' Joy said.

'Talking about obsession, what about Sidharth and Liss? They sounded pretty serious about each other.'

'Yeah. Even I was shocked. I remember, one night when Sidharth and Manika had drifted off to sleep, we found ourselves talking and Liss said . . .'

Joy's narration continued.

***

Just One of Those Nights

'Is he fine now?' I asked. Sidharth had spent the last few hours visiting the washroom repeatedly and made a plethora of noises from inside there. He had had a little too much to drink. He puked almost everything he had eaten for the last three days. Even for a regular drinker, mixing beer with whisky and vodka always spells disaster.

'I think so. He is sleeping now,' Liss said, sighing.

'I don't understand why the hell he keeps competing with you,' I said. It was one of the many times that he had lost a drinking contest to Liss. Still, he never gave up.

'Yes. He should know by now Indians can't drink as much as we do!' Liss smiled.

'That's nothing to be proud of!' I smirked.

'Sour grapes, Joy?'

'Not at all,' I said. 'Hey, you know this story is from the *Panchatantra*. Indian fantasy stories. We all read them when we were kids.'

'Oh. Like Harry Potter?'

'Something like that.' I said. 'But a lot older. Like, thousands of years older.'

'Hmm . . . Sidharth told me . . .'

'Nice. What else did he tell you?' I asked her.

'*Mai Hindi seekh raha hai,*' she said.

I burst out laughing. Not at the grammar of course, I instantly forgave her for that, but the way she said it, it was hilarious! I still remember that accent.

'*What!*' she said.

'No nothing,' I said. 'It's just very cute and it's *Mai Hindi seekh rahi hu,* since you are a girl. I know the gender is a little hard to get in our language, but the way you said it was charming!'

And then she made me repeat the sentence about ten times, checked and rechecked the verb, the tense and the gender in the sentence. She was really serious about it.

'You are not that bad. *Seriously.* It's considerable progress in three months. I am impressed!'

'Languages were my minor in graduation. I have a thing for them. *Muje accha lagti hai!*'

I didn't correct her this time. I didn't want to repeat the sentence another twenty times and make her understand the gender of things. Anyway, she was turning out to be too delightful for her size.

'Is that why you're learning Hindi? Your love for languages or your love for a guy who's shorter and considerably inferior looking?'

She laughed and said, 'I love him. And I love this country. When I grew up there in Hungary and then Poland, I had no family, nowhere to call home, but when I came here and I met you, your sister and Manika. All of you guys embraced me even after you knew what I used to do. For once in my life, I was a part of something. I had *friends*. And a loving guy by my side. I am just too selfish too lose all this,' she said, and looked out of the window to hide the tears streaming down her face.

'You are family here,' I said, not knowing what else to say.

'Thank you,' she said, wiped off her tears and smiled.

'You are always welcome. And it would be nice to have an ex-stripper in the family. Makes it exotic,' I winked. 'And maybe you can teach my future wife a few of your moves. That would be fun for me!'

'Right!' she said, paused and continued, 'Can I ask you something, if you don't mind?'

'We just established we are family, didn't we?' I said. 'Go ahead!'

'Do you love *her*? Manika?'

'C'mon,' I said, trying to hide the obvious.

'Kya tum Manika se pyaar karti ho?'

I suppressed a smile. 'Why do you ask that?'

'Because I think she does,' she said. 'I can sense it.'

'You're wrong, she doesn't. She has a boyfriend and she loves him and they are serious and committed. I really have no business spoiling what they have.'

'And yet, she is living with you?'

'That's because she likes it here. Plus we are all together. It's fun living here.'

'You think that's the reason?'

'I don't know. But she is happy with that guy and I don't want to ruin that for her. We were together before and I ruined it.'

'I think you had already ruined Manika for others,' she said. 'She told me that you were a great boyfriend while you were with her. She never stops talking about you.'

'Well yes, we were pretty awesome. I think we still are,' I mumbled.

'See,' she said and smiled at me.

'*What?*'

'Nothing,' she said and sipped on her coffee, still looking at me as if trying to hint at something. A little later, Sidharth came looking for Liss and they went off to sleep. I tossed and turned in bed for quite some time. What Liss had said kept troubling me.

Over the last few weeks, life had been *perfect*. There was nothing missing and I missed no one.

Was I too busy to notice that I was falling in love with her again? Was I too busy to realize that she was all I needed? *This can't be*, I told myself. I can't take a chance with her again; I ruin everything every time; I sort of have a hundred per cent record.

I had been selfish before and I hated what I'd done to her. I had given her way too many crying nights to give her any more of them. She had been happy with Ravi before. And she would be again, I tried to convince myself. I had no right to spoil it. I had to lose her to make sure she was happy.

Liss had unwittingly destroyed everything. She had put the last nail in the coffin. I had been avoiding thinking about Manika and me but she had now drilled it into my head!

The following days were troublesome and it only worsened after Liss and Sidharth left for Paris. Sidharth had to report to the university and register himself for the next semester, so they cut their trip short, and they took the first flight they could get from Delhi. Liss's words kept haunting me.

* * *

'*Don't fucking tell me!*' *I said.* '*Did you tell her you wanted another shot?*'

'*I wanted to. It was hard not to love her and want her to be around me,*' *Joy said.*

'*Don't tell me you spoiled her relationship with Ravi, you retarded fuck-up!*' *I exclaimed.*

The door creaked and both of us looked at it slam against the wall, and she entered in all her splendour. She came in and smiled at us.

'*Yes, he is,*' *she said.* '*He is retarded. Ask me! I have been putting up with his bullshit for the last so many years now.*'

'*Hi, Manika!*' *I said and went and hugged her. She looked as stunning as ever. She is one of those girls you don't even feel jealous of because she is so far ahead of you in terms of looks, panache and style that all you can do is look at her, smile, admire and wish you would be like her. That's a lot of expectation from a girl. But Manika evoked such emotions.*

'*Hi, Neeti,*' *she said,* '*and hi, baby. I have been calling you since morning, where is your phone?*'

'*I don't know,*' *Joy said as he looked around for his cell phone.* '*Oh, it's on silent. I am sorry, baby.*'

'*Shut up, Joy. This "baby" business won't work on me. What*

214

the heck were you so busy with?' Manika scolded him. It sounded so sweet, mostly because, for the first time, I had seen Joy at a loss for words. And scared, too.

'Nothing! I was just telling Neeti our story,' he said.

'Was he?' Manika asked.

'Yes, he was.' I said.

'Then it is fine,' she said and hugged Joy and they sat in front of me. They looked so much in love!

'So where had he reached?' she asked me.

'Where Liss left and he realized that he loved you,' I said.

'Continue,' Manika asked Joy.

'Why don't you tell her rest of it?' Joy said as he snuggled up to her.

'Yes! That should be fun,' I said. 'Why don't you continue, Manika?'

'If you insist! From the part where Liss left, right?' Manika said. 'Okay, so ever since they left, Joy had been behaving a little strangely.'

It was Manika's turn to start narrating.

***

Manika's Side

'The house looks a little empty without them doesn't it?' I said, as Joy looked around, clueless. He had been acting a little strange of late and I hadn't bothered asking why.

'Yes. It sure does, Manika,' he said, after a long pause.

I lay down on the couch and closed my eyes. Joy and I had spent the last night drinking but I still couldn't get any sleep. I checked my phone for any messages. *No messages*. It had been three days since Ravi had called or messaged me and I hadn't missed it or him for that matter. I hadn't missed the lack of communication for the last many, many days. Anyway, these days he called only to call me a slut or a whore, depending on how he felt that day. I don't blame him for that. It was my fault. But the day I told him that I would stay with Joy in Delhi, I knew that sooner or later it would be over between the two of us. And deep inside my heart, I wished that would come true.

Ravi had been great. He had been loyal and loving, and had never given me a single chance to complain, and for a moment, I thought I loved him, too. I had convinced myself that he was the guy I could be with. But it was just not to be.

As I heard somewhere, the heart wants what it wants. For all the time I was with Ravi, I tried my best to love him, recreate the magic I had with Joy, but it was never the same. I told myself that it would come with time, but it didn't. I wasn't even sure whether I still loved Joy. I was sure that I hated Joy and hated him a lot, but I wasn't sure if my love for him was greater than that.

The first day I heard Joy cry, I bled. I know it's stupid and uncalled for, but I reckon it was one of the worst days I had ever seen. And it wasn't because I couldn't see him cry. It was because I felt cheated. Joy had been seeing other girls and having fun but I always felt and thought that I was special. I used to think that I was the one he only truly loved, that I was the only one he would cry for, that no matter what happens, at the end of the day he would always come back to me.

But that seemed to have changed now. Joy was crying for someone *else*. I felt violated. I felt bad. And that was the day I finally felt that I had really lost him . . . forever. I had called up Neeti and she gave me the same picture. Just a few weeks? And this was his state of affairs? It was already shocking enough that he was doing this for someone else. I was *broken*. I couldn't help but be by his side. I had my questions to ask him. I wanted to grab him by his collar and ask him—what made him cry for a girl whom he didn't even love? What had she done that I hadn't? What was so special about this girl? I wanted answers! If not that, I just wanted to be with him, and see him through it, and understand what did I not do that this girl, Natasha, did.

Ravi had told me that he would never see my face again once I said I would not move out of Joy's apartment. He broke up with me, and though he said he wouldn't call or message, he kept doing that for weeks.

'You're a bad person and you don't deserve to be happy.'

That's what he said most of the times. But I was with the person I loved the most. So I didn't care.

I cried for the first few weeks that I was with Joy, and I realized that what I was doing to Ravi was outrageous, but after a very long time I was happy, truly happy. Despite the crying, the fights with Ravi and putting up with Joy's depressing ways, just seeing him every day, seeing him smile once in a while, seeing him wreck the house, seeing him try his hand at cooking again . . . it made me just so glad. It was back to the way it was always meant to be—Joy and Manika.

I used to tell Joy that Natasha wasn't worth it, and that he would find better girls in his life, and a whole lot of other things that I just hated telling him, but I still couldn't help feeling complete with him. Being around him *made* me complete. There were times I felt bad about myself that I needed an asshole like him near me to make me feel complete, a guy who didn't even care about me. But then, I was in *love*.

There were times I wished I could shake him and tell him how much I loved him, but I always feared what he would say. And deep in my heart, I would tell myself that he would fall in love with me again. I would pray for it, day after day, night after night.

A month passed and he had not. He said *nothing* about it.

He even asked me to move back to my apartment after he saw me crying once. More than Ravi, I was crying for myself . . . for the way I was. I had left a perfectly nice guy who loved me and had come to someone who didn't even care about me. There were some things that happened I wished he would see and realize that we were great as a couple, but blind as he was, he didn't. I too stayed shut.

The time I met Arnab and Sarah, I felt jealous. I wished he, too, would *see* me. Notice me. Hug me. And tell me that I was *the one*, but he didn't. The time Nisha met us at the school reunion and told us that we were an inspirational couple, I hoped it would get into some place inside his head and he would realize that we were meant to be together. There was no one I wanted more than him. Yet, there was no one who was less ignorant of my feelings. Things got worse when Sidharth and Liss went back to Germany. He asked me to move to my own place. The truth was that I didn't have a place in Delhi; I lived in a guest house for a few days close to his apartment and told him I had taken a flat nearby; he never asked further. I came from Bangalore just to live with him.

'I think you should move back to your own place,' Joy said.

'What?' I said, as my heart crushed into a million pieces. 'Joy, we have been through this before. I like it here. And Ravi doesn't have a problem. I told you that, didn't I?'

'I don't think he doesn't have a problem.'

'He doesn't. Didn't I say I handled the situation? Or is it you who wants me out of here?'

'No! I *love* you here. It's great. But then, now that I am fine, I might start dating, and you being around kills my chances, you see. No girl would like to compete with you,' he winked and I cried inside.

'Oh, so you want to date again?' I said, trying not to change my expression.

'Maybe,' he said.

'Fine then. I will move out tomorrow.'

'Great,' he said and turned up the volume of the television. He always did that whenever he wanted to avoid a conversation with me. But this was the first time he had done such a thing during my stay there. How on earth had he become so *cold?* I went to my room and locked it from the inside. I cursed myself till I was hoarse, and cried myself to sleep. The next day, we hardly talked and I shifted to a friend's place. With every box that I packed, sealed and carried out of that house, I lost a part of my life. It was like picking up the last pieces of my life. I cried a lot that day. And he didn't even notice.

* * *

'You are such a bastard, Joy,' I said. 'Manika was so much in love with you and this is how you treated her?'

'I always say the same thing,' Manika said.

'I didn't know what she felt about me! And the only reason I kicked her out was because I couldn't bear the fact that she had a guy! I wanted to tell her that I loved her, but I couldn't! It was killing me. Every time her phone beeped and she went inside to talk to Ravi, it killed me. I couldn't take it. I couldn't take the fact that some other guy had control over her life. That she shared something with that guy that she couldn't share with me. It was very hard for me to bear all this.'

'And it killed me when I moved out,' Manika said.

'Awww,' Joy said, and hugged her tight.

'Sweet couple you are, the both of you,' I said. 'Anyway, so what happened after she moved out?'

'The same thing all over again! I went into depression. Only this time, there was no Manika to take care of me. She had started ignoring me,' Joy said.

'I had no choice,' Manika said.

'So basically, both of you knew that you loved each other and still remained away from each other? Must have been terrible, right?' I said.

'Mind-numbingly terrible,' Joy said.

'More for me,' Manika said.

'Fuck you.'

'Fuck you,' Manika said.

'Okay, you can do that later, now why don't you both tell me, one by one, how it was for you to stay away?' I said. 'Manika, first you . . .'

Manika started narrating her side of the story.

* * *

Manika's Sob Story

I didn't think it would be this hard. Or at least I had wished it would not be. I spent my days trying not to cry. You are allowed to be selfish in love, right? I was. And I wanted him. What is so wrong in that? What was so wrong in me expecting that he would at least see that I was in love with him? At least acknowledge the fact that I loved him.

No sign whatsoever.

What's more—after the first few days of separation, he hadn't even bothered to call or ask how I was. Just a few messages wishing me good morning, good night at times, that was all. How could he be so heartless? I left *everything* for him. And this is how he repaid me. I was a fool to be in love with him.

I stayed indoors weekend after weekend, on the couch, watching romantic flicks with happy endings that made me sicker. But there was nothing else that I could do. The ashtrays kept piling up with cigarette butts and the flat was filled with the stench of cigarettes.

Ravi called up a few times and I abused him every time that happened. I was so miserable that it felt good someone else was miserable like me, too. And surprisingly, I had stopped feeling bad about him. *Why should I?* Nobody felt bad about *me*!

But Ravi realized that something was wrong with me. His project brought him to Delhi, and the first thing he did after landing here was to see me. That guy really loved me. I cursed myself to have fallen for the wrong guy.

'You look terrible,' he said.

'I know,' I said. 'You look good, though.'

'Look Manika. I don't know what it is with you and Joy, but I am sorry for all the past months. I was just very angry. And you have to forgive me for it. It was a shock to me. I was in love with you!'

'Hmm.'

'After all that we shared, one fine day, you just walked away from me and went back to him. It was really too much for me to take,' he said. It looked like he would start crying.

'I am sorry, Ravi,' I said. 'You're one of the nicest guys I have ever met. I am so sorry for whatever happened between us.'

'Manika . . . I am sorry for all the name-calling and abuses. You know I didn't mean them. I was just very angry and frustrated with you. But do you have to do this? Joy? Are you sure of what you're doing?'

'Yes. Being with anyone else would be unfair. I hope you understand,' I said and held his hand. I hoped he would feel better.

'I do. I mean, that's what I tell myself every day,' he said and half chuckled.

'Anyway, enough of this depressing talk. What's up with you? Any new girl in your life?' I asked, trying to lighten up the mood.

'Ummm . . .'

'A pause? Which means there is?' I said.

'Not really. But when you left me, all crushed and crying and angry, there was a girl in my office who took care of me. And I am beginning to like her. It's too early to say anything, but let's see,' he said.

And believe me, I was so relieved! It was like a huge boulder off my shoulder. I wished and prayed they would fall in love.

'So? What's her name? How does she look? How is she?' I asked.

'I promise I will tell you when something concrete happens.'

'Fine. Fine,' I said.

'So, what's with you? And Joy?'

'Maybe he really doesn't love me anymore and I was fooling myself.'

'I really don't get you, Manika. You left our perfectly good life for this uncaring bastard! On a whim? On a hope?' he asked, exasperated. I didn't blame him.

'Ravi, this is all I want, and this is what can keep me happy,' I said.

'I am sorry. I am sure someday I will get what you are trying to say,' he said. 'But if you love him so much, why don't you tell him so?'

'I don't have an answer to that.'

'You're strange, Manika.'

'I know,' I said and smiled at him.

We shared a quiet coffee together and he left later that evening. I thanked him for coming and we promised each other that we would still be friends.

The days rolled by and nothing changed in the situation between the *bastard* and me. All the effort that I had been putting in the office in the first month was going to waste now. I wasn't working. I spent hours at the coffee house puffing cigarettes with other non-performing assets of the company, thinking about him. Surprisingly, it seemed like all the time between our break-up and our coming back together never existed. No time without him was worth remembering.

There were times I used to sit at home and wonder what had happened to me. I was a strong, independent girl who used to have a field day mocking all the girls who fell in love, broke their hearts and ended up spending their days crying . . . and now I was one of them. I was in self-destruct mode.

During those days, I resisted the temptation to call up Joy and tell him what he meant to me, and what an asshole he was, but I didn't want to embarrass myself. *Maybe he has already started dating someone*, I said to myself.

The depression from being away from him was like a disease. It kept getting worse. Even my kid sister got worried this time. After so many years, we had changed places. She was taking care of me now. She asked me why I couldn't tell him that I loved him.

'TELL HIM? That's the last thing I will ever do! Can't he fucking *see*? After all that he did to me, I left my guy and stayed with him just so that he could get over that girl he was so obsessed with . . . and he can't see *that*!' I had said, agitatedly. She offered to stay there for the night, but I made her go. It was anyway embarrassing to cry for a guy in front of my baby sister.

***

'Sad,' I said. 'Joy? Do you think you can beat that?'

'Me? No,' he said and his eyes welled up. 'Come here,' he said to Manika and kissed her on the lips.

'You really killed me then,' Manika said, sobbing softly.

'I am so sorry for that,' Joy said. 'If only I knew . . .'

'How could you not know?' Manika said. 'You always knew what I had in mind before I could say it . . . What happened then?'

'I am sorry. And why didn't you just tell me?'

'Why couldn't you see?'

'I was blind,' he said and hugged her close.

'GUYS!' I said. 'Now don't make me cry . . . and Joy, continue . . .'

'Okay,' he said. 'I will keep the crying part to the minimum. It's very depressing.'

'Fine. Whatever. Just go ahead!'

'Umm . . .'

Joy continued. . .

***

227

Joy and His Sob Story

When Manika left, it felt like the world crashed around me. It was different this time. Not like the time Natasha left me. In her case, I just missed the person. In Manika's case, I missed what I was with her, what we were together and what people thought of us together.

That night with Arnab and Sarah, I could see envy in their eyes. The day with Nisha, I felt the blood rush to my head when she said that we were an inspiring couple, and they wanted their story to be like ours, perfect and beautiful.

She was with Ravi now. And it didn't seem she would ever come back to me again. She had harped in the past about how nice and dependable Ravi was and I couldn't take that happiness away from her. It pained me every day to imagine the love of my life with someone else, but that was what it had to be. I had my chance and I dropped it. I had the love of the prettiest and the most charming girl I had ever seen in my life in my palms and I dropped it.

It sucked. There were so many times that I had wanted to tell her that I loved her. I wondered about a million times how the conversation would go. I would say I love her. She would say that I was just saying it because I was fresh out of a break-up. I would start begging. And she would ask me to *fuck off*. I was better off *not* telling her.

I called her for a few days and she picked up only a few of my calls. Some days later, I stopped calling her since it was getting tougher to talk to her and not tell her how much I *loved* her. I even wrote bullet points on a sheet of paper and kept it near the phone.

- Love you.
- Sorry.
- Be a part of my life.
- I am a fool to have let you go.
- You're a princess to me; I will always treat you like one.
- Your smile means everything to me.
- I don't want any guy around you. Ever.
- Break up with Ravi.

But I never had the courage to pick up the phone and tell her these things. The time was gone and I had lost the moment. It had all come back to haunt me. I used to spend hours those days looking at our old pictures and videos, reminiscing about how good and happy we were together. How we spent our days locked up in a small room whispering sweet nothings to each other, how days passed without us knowing what was happening outside the little, warm and cosy room we slept in, how we were so dangerously content in each other's company, and how we really pissed off people around us because we were so much in love!

~

* * *

'I think you should have just told me.' Manika said.
'I know I should have,' Joy said and continued.

* * *

I used to lie on my bed like a pig every day and spend hours on Facebook checking her profile. Manika was never too much of a Facebook person and never updated anything. Though it was the first profile I checked every day.

But then, as luck would have it, one fine day, or the finest day of my wretched life, I spotted a news update on my Facebook profile. Usually I never look too much into them, but that day, by a stroke of luck, I spotted something.

Surbi is friends with Ravi Kadyan. Manika had liked the post.

Surbi was the girl I had dated for a couple of months just after I had joined MDI, Gurgaon after my job at the engineering firm. She had dumped me for some other guy and that was from where I had picked up the story of the third book! She had been my muse. How could I have forgotten her?

And Ravi was, well—*Manika's* Ravi!

I sighed and wondered how small the world was, how much it had shrunk, and yet Manika and I were apart. I clicked through Surbi's profile out of boredom and noticed that she was interning at the same firm where Ravi had been working for many years. Later that night, I was checking her updates and noticed that within the six hours that she and Ravi had been friends, she had liked almost all his profile pictures and commented on dozens of them. I wondered why she would gush over Ravi so much, but then she had always been a bit of a, with all due respect, slut.

For the first time in months, I logged into Facebook chat and I saw that Surbi was online. I thanked God that Surbi had dumped me and not the other way around. I could still ping her and not get cursed. I was the *victim* in the relationship!

Me: Hi Surbi!
Surbi: Hi Joy.
Me: Long time. Where are you working?
Surbi: Colgate. I heard you are interning in Delhi, right? So what else?
Me: Nothing. You tell me. How is office? Any new hot guys? Or still with the older one?
Surbi: Naah, I broke up with him.
Me: So anyone in office?
Surbi: Naah.
Me: C'mon! Don't lie! There must be someone. Are the guys in your office blind that they don't hit on you?
Surbi: Hmmm . . . actually there is this one guy. I find him cute! ☺
Me: Oh, you do ? Who is he? TELL ME!
Surbi: No one. A senior of mine. We just went on one date. Don't know if he even likes me!
Me: I am sure he does. Who is he? Paste me the link!
Surbi: Wait.

She typed and my heart pounded in anticipation. I was already imagining scenarios where Surbi seduces Ravi, and Ravi ends up cheating on Manika, and I am the good guy who makes everything all right.

Surbi: Here. http://www.facebook.com/pages/phputr/ 116852198388214?ref=ts

I opened the link; it was Ravi.

Me: Nice guy. Is he single?

I typed, and hoped and hoped she would ensnare him and make him cheat on Manika.

Surbi: Since the last two months, I guess. His girl left him for her ex-guy. He doesn't talk much about it. Poor guy.☹ She must be a slut. But Ravi is really nice. ☺

WHAT!

Me: Are you certain? Do you know who his girl was?
Surbi: Nope. He has asked me not to talk about it. So I don't ask him. ☹
Me: Does he know that you dated me Surbi?
Surbi: Nope. For other people, I never dated you. You know, I regret you. ☺
Me: lol. ☺
Surbi: What about you?
Me: Nothing much. Anyway. BRB. GTG. Catch you later. Bye.

I went offline.

And read the conversation again. I saw the profile again. And I saw the comments again. And then, I peeped into Ravi's friends list and wondered why I hadn't done that before, which like most guys' profiles was unlocked.

I came across a series of posts that were borderline suicidal, and there were songs about betrayal and cheating and lost love. I flipped down the laptop, picked up the car keys and drove like a madman to Manika's house, my head bursting with countless possibilities and situations. Fuck, was this really happening. This was *fucking* happening.

I ran up the flight of the stairs. I jumped steps, knocked over people and stood outside her door, my head bursting and my heart ready to pop out of my chest. I knocked on her door.

'Who's it?' she said.

'It's me,' I said.

***

'COOL!' I shrieked out.

    'Very cool,' Joy said.

    'Go on . . .'

    'I will let Manika continue,' he said.

    'Okay,' Manika said. 'This can get a little nasty.'

    'I love nasty,' I said.

    'So . . .,' she continued her narration.

***

Manika and Joy

As a habit, I used to check Ravi's profile almost every day, after I checked Joy's. I saw Ravi's new pictures. A girl had liked and commented on every picture of his. She wasn't all that bad. The comments were obviously very mushy, but it didn't matter a bit. Far from being jealous, I was a little relieved. They would look good together. I said a little prayer for them in my mind.

I switched onto somebody else's profile. It was the third weekend straight that I was staying at home and watching television. Early morning cigarette. Then answer the calls that nature made. Skipping the bath. A tub full of pasta. And an entire day of television. The usual schedule.

Just as I was on the third consecutive episode of *Friends* or *Homeland* or *Supernatural* that morning, there was a knock on the door. I wasn't really expecting anyone. I hadn't for long. I hadn't called anyone, so I just assumed it would be the cleaning lady.

'Who's it?' I shouted out from the sofa itself.

'It's me,' the voice from the other side said.

Joy? Fuck! What is he doing here!

I jumped from the couch and looked around; the house was a mess. I looked in the mirror. I was still in my three-day-old sweatpants, my hair was dishevelled, eyes were puffed—I looked like an ugly witch from Harry Potter! I prioritized the things I had to and allotted time to it.

- Stuff the clothes and everything in one room. Lock the room. 15 seconds.
- Wash face. 15 seconds.
- Lip balm. 15 seconds.
- Run to the door and shout that I was coming. 15 seconds.
- Blusher. 15 seconds.
- Throw the utensils in the sink and close the door. 15 seconds.
- Run to the door and shout that I was coming. 15 seconds.
- Brush hair. 15 seconds.

Two minutes and I was done with everything. I checked myself in the mirror for one last time. *Not bad*, I patted myself. Though I was not in the best of what I could have been, but not bad either.

'Hey,' I said, as I opened the door.

'Hi. Took you long?' he asked.

'Oh,' I faked a yawn. '. . . just got up . . .'

'You look great,' he said, as he entered the flat. It seemed like a genuine comment. It seemed like the blusher and the lip balm had worked.

'Thank you. So do you,' I said.

He stood there for a while and stared at me. That intense stare was somewhat familiar. I didn't know what to make of it because it seemed so out of place. He came close, held my hand and caressed my fingers with his. It was really abrupt. I didn't know what to make of that either.

'Joy,' I whispered his name out when he brushed his fingers against my lips and whispered *shut up*. He brushed away the hair from my face and blew out air to push it back. His breath sent tingles down my spine as he pulled me to himself. He stared at me with his teary eyes, he leaned on me, laid his lips on mine and pressed. I surrendered. He kissed me. My lips were ensconced in his. I kissed him back. There were tears in his eyes. As they were in mine.

'Joy,' I said feebly. I felt a strange sensation. It wasn't lust. His touch, his eyes, and his breath on mine—it felt like an emotional orgasm. I was overwhelmed. Tears streamed down my cheeks as his strong arms wrapped themselves around me. I was weak and I didn't want to fight. I was his. My heart, my mind, and my body—they were all his to take, to love, to leave. I didn't care.

The kiss lasted for a long time. My mind went into flashback of everything that I had shared with him. From the first day to this one.

'What?' I said, as he pushed me towards the couch. Words barely escaped my mouth. I was lost. He picked me up and laid me down on the couch.

'Shut up,' he said. His hands gripped both sides of my neck and pulled me further onto him. He looked at me with his smouldering eyes, as if he would never take them off me. His lips and tongue wandered all over my lips and I gave out a long moan as he started to lick my ear and then bit into it. My heart started to skip beats and my nails clawed into this shirt, which I found myself taking off within the next few seconds. I was divided in two. One part wanted to hug him and never let him go. Cry and tell him that I wanted to be with him. It wanted to tell him that he meant everything to me. The other part wanted to feel him, love him and make love to him, even if it was wrong to do so.

Soon, he took off his shirt, and I could see his chiselled body on top of me. He was *perfect*. His hands crawled below, undid my sweat uppers, and threw them on the ground, his tongue never breaking contact with my neck as he fed on me. My toenails curled as he slowly and steadily had me naked in front of him. It felt so *right*.

He drew back and stared at me, as if it was the last time we would be together. Then he rolled on top of me slowly, his passionate eyes never losing sight of my body. His outstretched hand slowly reached my face and he ran his fingers down along its contour, over my lips where they paused for a few seconds when he bent over me. He kissed me lightly. His hand slowly moved over my neck and then grabbed it from behind while his other hand grasped one of my hands. His hold was steady and strong. He pinned my hands on the couch armrest and let his teeth hurt every part of my body until I screamed aloud. The pain that came from him only made me love him more. It always made me realize how much he meant to me.

He feasted on me as if it was what he had waited for all his life. I went into periodical trances every time he touched and entered places and made me moan and struggle in his arms. He was strong, savage, and fighting him was a waste and I didn't even *want* to. He ravaged me; his hands and his body ruled every part of mine and blocked every other sensation. I was lost in him, his grunts, his thrusts and his love. He took me as his own, and embraced me in an intertwining spiral of love and lust. Our bodies, naked and writhing, rolled over on to the ground as he went on to make me feel like I had never felt before. His force had me in tears of ecstasy as I shouted and begged him to hurt me more. I wished it would never end as I clasped his back with my legs . . .

When done, he lay panting with his head on my shoulder and my legs wrapped around his lower back which just refused to let his body go . . . In those moments, I didn't know if what had happened was for real or not, but I had never felt this content before. For the next few minutes, I tried to talk, but nothing escaped my lips, as we both lay totally spent. He rested there for quite some time, after which he looked up and kissed me on my forehead. He kept doing this repeatedly.

'How did you know?' I asked him as he continually kissed me on my left cheek while caressing my hair. Frankly speaking, my hair still stood on end for what he had just done to me, and I was still numb.

'How did I know what?'

'Don't play with me. How did you know that Ravi and I were through?' I asked, and ran my hands through his hair. It had been ages since I had done that and I had forgotten how great it felt. I hated the fact that he had cut his hair short but I never told him.

'How can you say that I knew?' he asked.

'Because you wouldn't have kissed me unless I was yours. You were never like that,' I said.

'You remember Surbi?' he asked, as he stared deep into my eyes. I melted in his arms.

'*Surbi?* Oh, the girl you dated? The muse for the third book?'

'Have you seen Ravi's profile of late?' he asked. He was being incredibly cute. His lips never left my skin.

'Oh . . . shit . . . don't tell me! *That* Surbi? And Ravi! I saw but never realized that she was that girl!'

'Yes!'

'And you knew I would be waiting for you?'

'I hoped with my life that you would be,' he said and kissed me on the lips.

'But . . . what if—'

'Let's not live with what-ifs. This time, it's for life.'

'You said that the last time, too.'

'Now I know what life is without you and I don't want that life. I want *you*,' he kissed me.

'Are you sure?'

'I have a ring in my pocket,' he said and looked at me. 'Yes, it's imaginary, but I think it will do for the time being.'

'What? *Really?*' I said. 'Let's get engaged!'

'Damn.'

'*Jerk!*' I said.

'But I am true to my word. From this moment on, you are *everything* to me. Every time I use the word *love*, it will be for you. Every time I dedicate a song, it will be for you. Every time I hold a hand, it will be yours. Every time I yearn to hear a voice, it will be yours. I am yours, for life.'

'You'd better be,' I said.

'I prepared that speech! And you could just come up with *you'd better be*?'

'I just made out with you, Joy. Isn't that enough?' I winked.

'Well, I can make do with that,' he smiled and kissed me.

I kissed him back. And we kissed our best. This time as we kissed, I swore I would never let him go. He was everything to me. And I was his. He was my reason to live, to laugh, and to breathe.

There was a lot of crying that night, I distinctly remember. We told each other a million things about what we loved about each other and we kissed a zillion times for each one of them.

'You know, I had missed making out with you,' he said, exhausted once more.

'I wish I could say the same,' I winked.

'Funny,' he said. 'But why didn't you just tell me that you had broken up with him for me?' he asked me.

'Why didn't you? And how could I have after the way you left me? Take a chance again and get my heart trampled over like you do every single time.'

'You could have tried!' he said.

'I wanted to, but I wasn't strong enough to take another heartbreak. Do you have any idea how many nights I have spent thinking and crying over an asshole like you?'

'Let's not count. Let's count the days we will spend loving each other. Starting today. That's a much better picture, isn't it?'

'It is,' I said. 'It sure is.'

And we were back. Like we had been. Like it was always meant to be. Seemed like even though *we had been single for a while . . . we had never stopped being lovers.*

‘Aw!’ I said. ‘So sweet. So, this is it, huh? Joy? This is the end?’

   ‘It feels more like the beginning,’ he said.

   ‘It better be,’ she said.

   ‘Once bitten, twice shy,’ he said and hugged her close. ‘And I have the best thing in the world with me. Why try anything else when you know?’

   ‘That better be it,’ Manika said and kissed him.

   They were not the only ones who had tears in their eyes. And this is how they celebrated their second *first anniversary. I was a witness. An unwelcome witness.*

***

Epilogue

After he told me the story, Joy kept asking me for many days if I would write something on it or not. Especially since I had not taken any notes at all. But days passed and I saw these two falling more in love every passing day. Joy had turned out to be the kind of boyfriend girls discuss with their other girlfriends. I just *had* to write it. It may not be something special where the guy gets the girl after fighting off a rich tyrannical father, but it is a lesson on how it could go terribly wrong if you don't recognize the importance of love and don't respect it.

Joy realized right in time and made amends, but he had always been a lucky bastard. Still, there had been a rather strong chance that he would have fallen flat on his face and not found anyone. Now that would have been sad, wouldn't it?

So, don't lose your faith in love. It's there. It's around. There is someone for everyone. You might have fallen for the wrong girls and the wrong guys, or thought that the right girl was the wrong one, but then again, that doesn't mean the search . . . or realization . . . ends. Who knows—after all, the guy who just walked past you might end up spending the next Valentine's Day with you!

As for me, I have to rush now. I have a date. Nice guy. Who knows, he might be the one! *Fingers crossed!*

Another Epilogue

'*Neeti is a great storyteller. Nothing in this book should be considered reliable or accurate!*'

—Joy Datta

Acknowledgements

I don't have a lot of people to thank, since not many knew I had decided to write a book. However, there are still people without whom this book could never have been written.

First, I would like to thank Joy Datta for being candid enough to share his story with me. He has always been a good friend and without his help, this book would not have been possible. I thank him for helping me to write this book.

Sachin Garg, for he is such a lucky charm and an extremely capable guide. Maanvi Ahuja, another lucky charm.

I would also like to thank a few other people who had always been around and supported me throughout my journey—Jyoti Anand, Samarth Anand, Samvedna Anand, Anumodit Chaturvedi, Abhishek Choudhary, Nandita Samant, Shikha Sharma, Komal Milap . . . and others whose names I might have skipped.

Last but not the least—I thank our extended families for they have been very supportive.

—Neeti Rustagi